**Adel Esmat**, born in the Gharbiya Governorate of Egypt in 1959, graduated in philosophy from the Faculty of Arts of Cairo's Ain Shams University in 1984. He lives in Tanta, in the Nile Delta, and works as a library specialist in the Egyptian Ministry of Education.

**Mandy McClure** is the translator of *Arab Women Writers: A Critical Reference Guide* (AUC Press, 2008) and co-translator of *The Traditional Crafts of Egypt* (AUC Press, 2016). She lives in Cairo.

T0346355

# Tales of Yusuf Tadrus

Adel Esmat

Translated by
Mandy McClure

hoopoe

AN IMPRINT OF AUC PRESS

First published in 2018 by
Hoopoe
113 Sharia Kasr el Aini, Cairo, Egypt
420 Fifth Avenue, New York, 10018
www.hoopoefiction.com

Hoopoe is an imprint of the American University in Cairo Press
www.aucpress.com

Exclusive distribution outside Egypt and North America by I.B.Tauris & Co Ltd., 6
Salem Road, London, W4 2BU

Dar el Kutub No. 11309/17
ISBN 978 977 416 860 4

Dar el Kutub Cataloging-in-Publication Data

Esmat, Adel
      Tales of Yusuf Tadrus / Adel Esmat.—Cairo: The American University
  in Cairo Press, 2018.
      p.        cm.
      ISBN 978 977 416 860 4
      1. Arabic Fiction—Translation into English
      892.73

1 2 3 4 5    22 21 20 19 18

Designed by Adam el-Sehemy
Printed in the United States of America

For Ibrahim Philips and Ashraf Michel

I said to the almond tree, "Speak to me of God." And the almond tree blossomed—Nikos Kazantzakis, *Report to Greco*

# Yusuf Tadrus says:

Yesterday I dreamed of the resurrection rite.

The light was dim, coming from candles set in niches along the length of the wall. The silence was heavy, save for the faint sound of chants. There were about five of us. We were walking in a long line and wearing flowing gallabiyas, like the light ones farmers wear, made of coarse cotton. I was terrified. All I could think was: How had I gotten here and who brought me and there must be some mistake.

We entered a spacious, square room with no furnishings but a linen rug spread out on the floor. The abbot stood next to a small pulpit. We stood in front of him in a row, like in a morning roll call. He gestured for us to lie down on the rug. We obeyed as if hypnotized.

I was still baffled, thinking about how I'd gotten there. I knew it was too late and there was no going back. The sound of the chants grew louder and my thoughts deserted me. Only the fear remained. It was too late to turn back. I had to submit to my fate. Maybe my life here would be better.

We lay down, our backs to the ground and faces to the ceiling. I saw only darkness. I felt a sheet thrown over us, covering us from head to toe. I smelled the scent of linen and felt its roughness on my face. The chants grew louder. Funeral rites were performed, every step of them. I submitted to them. Then the voices gradually grew distant and a silence fell, so heavy you were afraid to breathe. Then the breath vanished and I no longer felt anything.

I don't know how long I stayed in the darkness of the veil. There was no time there. Silence and darkness. The veil lifted in a blur. The light shone from two candles on a high shelf. I struggled to orient myself, and then I heard prayer chants, as if the sun were shining. The flame of the two candles was fixed in place, as if there were no air here.

We stood in a line again, and the abbot descended two stairs holding scissors. After pronouncing each of our names, he left a mark on our heads with the scissors. When he approached me, his face was stony, lifeless, except for an overwhelming radiance in his eyes. He impressed the mark on my head and pronounced my name: Girgis. We began walking in the same line into a dark corridor, met with candles flickering in niches in the far distance. I couldn't look behind me. When I tried to remember my first name, I couldn't. I tried to recall anything about my former life and found only emptiness, as if everything I'd lived before had been completely erased.

# Yusuf Tadrus says:

MY MOTHER WAS A MEMBER of the Holy Bible Association. Every month she was tasked with collecting contributions from all over the city. That was in the mid-1960s—the city wasn't like it is now. I still remember al-Nadi Street with a child's eye: the open space carpeted in sunlight that lit up the asphalt and made the houses sparkle, flooding the dried flame trees, the white wall of the club, and the footpaths I could see through the iron bars of the wall. The silence was thick, like the neighborhood was encased in glass. We'd climb the stairs in a new building, cool, the apartments tucked away behind gleaming doors evoking an air of velvet, different from the earthy air of the alley where we lived. My mother would knock on the door. A slim man would greet us and welcome her, taking his receipt and giving her the monthly contribution. We'd stop by doctors' clinics, law offices, shop owners, and merchants. Every month we'd make the rounds of the city.

I discovered my love of light on those trips. And I got my fill of the story of my birth. Every month, I'd listen to a life account my mother had told dozens of times. How she had dedicated herself to the Lord, but her father had insisted on marrying her off at the age of thirty. She had a hard time getting pregnant—the pregnancy wouldn't fix itself in her womb—and she went to monasteries and churches. When the pregnancy finally came to term and she was on the verge of giving birth, she learned that pain is the Lord, and she loved her life and her pain, and gave birth to me.

This story left me with a vague restlessness; an uncomfortable feeling that my existence on the earth was a momentous happening, as if all those events and destinies that preceded it were staged for a certain purpose, so that this birth could take place. The story held a burden the thoughtless child did not wish to bear. There was something in it that weighed on my spirit. I tried to evade it all the time, but it dogged me. A ghost that inhabited my psyche and settled in. The story complicated my sense of self and left me with a nagging feeling that I was pledged to something I had to fulfill. It was as though I had to make some sort of sacrifice, as if my existence was not rightfully mine.

My mother's tale was dreary and I didn't like it. I distracted myself by observing light and shadow, and my love of light grew in the escape from the oppressive story of my birth.

My mother was a woman of considerable girth. When climbing the stairs, her joints ached, but she considered it a toll she had to pay. Suffering purifies; it rids people of sins they'd committed long ago. She would walk slowly, reciting in a low voice humanity's journey since the first sin. This slowness and her hushed voice let me contemplate shapes. These images were impressed clearly on my mind, as if they were part of a novel I'd once read.

Her labor and perseverance as she climbed the stairs held an acceptance of pain and a desire for sacrifice, her tribute of suffering that gladdened her soul. She had toiled in her life and it took her five years to have children, a boy and a girl. The association was her place for sacrifice, which she had to do in penance for an old sin. Our salvation is dependent on every individual offering up his or her measure of suffering.

At the end of the day, we'd return to the association to turn in the money we'd collected. I'd leave my mother and head for the workshops connected to the association's office. The place was an orphanage, and the donations were collected for the workshops: needlework for the girls and textile weaving for the boys. My infatuation began in that place. Every person has his own secret. It might not be a secret, but he carries it in his soul like a special jewel, a longing, compartments—I call them interior compartments. One feels all the time that this secret is what endows life with meaning. If he confesses it, he will have revealed his inner self. You won't believe it, but I know that's what makes you stand in front of the unfamiliar emotion in my paintings.

The carpet-weaving workshop was my secret. The wooden loom, the master preparing the yarn—the warp and the weft—and the pictures the yarn would later form. Sometimes I left the images midway and would return the next day to find a full carpet, as if a sorcerer had finished them. There was a stark contrast between, on the one hand, the vertical and horizontal strands, the gloom of the workshop, and the rough hands that arranged the yarn, and on the other the lovely images on the carpet. I couldn't believe that these delightful figures were the product of that tedious, daylong process. I wouldn't believe it until I'd seen the picture take shape.

My mother wouldn't let me stay, not even once, to see the picture come to completion. The unfinished images kept me awake. They made me rush through the collection errand so I could get back to the weaving workshop.

So I created my own myth. I thought that invisible creatures lived in the workshop. At night, after the doors were locked, they would awaken and start to draw and color, putting magical touches on linens and carpets. They would give the color red its warmth and to birds their abrupt movements in flight, making them more beautiful than the birds that would suddenly take flight from the top of the dome of the railway station.

That was my secret, and I lived it, which probably baffles you. My problem became how to stay longer. How could I hide in the workshop to see the creatures awaken and do their work?

One day I hid behind a door. They locked up the workshop and the association, and darkness fell. My heart beat violently. The silence had an energy that touched my soul and whetted my imagination. I saw transparent creatures like a fog come out of their hiding places and move on tiptoe. The windows were high up, a faint light penetrating them, and I felt the yarn move. I was afraid and screamed. I screamed and screamed, until a worker at the orphanage came and let me out, by then nearly comatose. After that I saw my mother crying, her eyes red, and I knew she'd looked everywhere for me.

I was ill for a long time. Fear is an illness I still haven't recovered from. During the fever, I heard the recitation of incantations and the voices of priests, and I felt the fog of church courtyards and my mother carrying me on her shoulder. I'd hear snippets of conversation about Yusuf, who'd been possessed by a species of jinn. Yusuf had been possessed. Imagine! They were right. I've been possessed ever since.

I didn't completely recover. After I regained consciousness, I started thinking about how to set up a loom in the house. After numerous attempts, it became clear that it was difficult. I couldn't bear the failure and cried for a whole night. My infatuation with the pictures on the carpets and kilims produced by the association's workshop persisted. They weren't pictures of saints or monks. They were pictures of birds, animals, and small thickets of vegetation, but the feeling that enveloped them was indescribable. The magic of the colors imbued the images with joy, and the joy safeguarded the secret.

I don't know when those images took shape as a secret. When did the trips to collect the contributions and the images from the carpet-weaving workshop become an interior light? You won't believe me if I tell you that the sunlight that I see with the old clarity gives me strength; it illuminates a patch in my depths. What led me to lock it up, like a lamp that would be extinguished if I spoke of its existence? And here I am now, speaking of it, so it can be snuffed out. I'm tired of its interior light, tired of keeping it inside me. I should let it light up a place broader than that darkness. Maybe in the open space it will shine more brightly.

When I was fourteen, I started collecting the monthly contributions in my mother's stead. People had come to know me. Their respect for her was imprinted in the way they treated me. They'd always ask about her kindly and say they'd drop by to visit. She left a sweet feeling behind, and love. I remember her whisper, as if she were talking to herself, when we'd approach a clinic or a home. This is Doctor Munir Girgis—his father was a goldsmith and he's a good man. Once he donated enough bolts of fabric to wrap a skyscraper. That's the shop of Foreman Farid—he spent his youth in Alexandria and came back with a large fortune. Small tales that looked for the bright side in people.

# Yusuf Tadrus says:

MARY LABIB, THE ART TEACHER, was my first love. I hope you're not shocked by love stories. Your brother Yusuf loved and was loved everywhere he landed. It's my fate. Mary looked like the movie star Maryam Fakhr al-Din. Her hair fell on her shoulders with a slight flip at the end. I was young. Even so, I declared my love to her and asked her to marry me. At my uncle Subhi's apartment, in the old house, they all laughed. I was serious, crying.

"Yusuf's really in love," my mother said, puzzled. "His eyes are red."

The word *red* appealed to me. I headed to the bathroom mirror and looked at my face. My eyes weren't red, but they were dull. That person looked at me angrily in the tilted mirror and told me something inscrutable. I immediately understood that I had to guard my secrets. I knew matters of love and emotion had to be guarded like jewels. A simple moment in front of the mirror, but it was a brief insight from the questioning voices I hear at times to this day.

One day Mary gave me a sketchbook and a box of crayons. Mary Labib Dimyan. I'll never forget her name. I'll keep remembering the full name, its edges fringed by a clear scent, the primary-school balcony, the sun illuminating the sand-covered schoolyard, Mary exiting the art room, trailing a scent I'll never be able to pinpoint. She'll remain a living portrait: a translucent smile, a striped dress fitted at the waist, butter-colored shoes with stiletto heels, a click on the tiles whose melody I'd never mistake, not even once. She'll remain alive in my depths, saying, "Paint what you wish. Don't be afraid, paint."

Maybe I've associated painting with a lack of fear ever since. Over the years, the phrase was translated into "painting delivers you from fear." I'll keep painting whenever I'm afraid. I'll keep painting as long as I live to rid myself of fear, which gets thicker and darker the older I get. Even after the worries began to lift—after Michel went to America and Fadi went to work in the jewelers' district, and it was just me and Janette, face to face, after a tempestuous journey—the fear was there flickering behind the scenes, unshakable, like the lining of the human heart.

Painting does not rid a person of fear, but it makes fears trivial, tolerable. From the moment Mary said "Paint what you wish. Don't be afraid," painting has been the good thing in my life. Even though I've abandoned it for long spells, I never for a moment stopped thinking about it, as if Mary's words were secretly guiding me. How can a child's love for his teacher stay alive all these years? Humans are as wondrous as life.

I'll never stop contemplating the sight of her. Of course, I won't paint it—if I paint her, she'll die. I only paint fears so they'll die. But Mary—her, I will not paint. If I did, she would fade into a picture. I'll leave her there, alive in my conscious-ness, like a candle in the window of Our Lady the Virgin. I'll keep her alive as long as I am.

I was sitting on a chair next to the window, drawing. A teacher named Talla Farag passed by and looked at the paper.

"What's this, Mary?" she said, pointing to the figure I'd drawn. "Is all of that a person?"

"Shush. Be quiet," Mary said. Smiling at me, she said, "Go on, finish it." She lowered her face kindly, with an under-standing smile. I've looked for this feeling everywhere—a friendly smile that tells you to keep going; whatever happens, finish what's in your hand. There are no standards there. There's nothing but finishing. Finish what's in your hand and you'll make it.

Mary knew. Those coal-black, keen, encouraging eyes look down on me whenever I sit down to paint. From behind they encourage me: Keep going, don't be afraid. I'll never voluntarily paint her. However great my longing for her, I won't paint her.

In middle school, I hated drawing because of a supercilious teacher who used to curse our families. He made us clean up the art room and line up the paints and colors, everything brought to meticulous order. At the end of school, the art room had to be neatly arranged, ready for the inspector's visit.

But my desire to make my fears concrete in images continued to mutate and found other paths. After I returned from the collection errand, I occupied myself with drawing carpets and fashioning wooden boxes. From plaster I made guns and other things that fulfilled my desire to produce figures. That period of not drawing was difficult. I remember it as an unending summer. Tedium and hollering and a sense that there was nothing to do but give yourself over to the life of the alley.

# Yusuf Tadrus says:

MY MOTHER WOULD WAKE UP at six a.m., before everyone, my father asleep in the interior room and my sister Nadia tossing in her bed, as if sensing her mother had left the house. I'd feel her opening the door and leaving. In that pleasant drowsiness in the winter months, the sound of the door was both calming and rousing. She was awake, anxious to meet the day, going to fetch the morning beans and porridge, the *al-Akhbar* newspaper and *Sabah al-kheir* magazine.

I was devoted to *Sabah al-kheir*. I loved the elegant, delightful drawings by al-Labbad, Bahgoury, Bahgat, al-Leithi, and other illustrators. Of them all, I was especially devoted to George Bahgoury. I'd wait for his illustrations and spend a long time poring over them. I wanted to draw like them. One day I read a sentence that filled me with extraordinary vigor: "George Bahgoury paints from Paris."

Look, this sentence—"paints from Paris"—put a spell on me. A warmth and luminosity pervaded life there, on the other side. What's that? Oh, a painting drawn in Paris, filled with warmth and sun and frittering the days away.

Hope blossomed from that sentence. When would it be said "Yusuf Tadrus paints from Paris"? Would that day come? I had a lot of confidence in myself, and my sense that life would reward me was growing as I was, especially when I noticed that girls were attracted to me.

I started drawing again, imagining the Paris cafés that George drew. I drew the things he did as if I were him, as if I lived in Paris. A lesson in identification that would later help me understand things—understand the spirit of the chairs, tables, stones, and windows. I would have secret ties with things from that moment. I'd befriend the lamps, glasses, empty bottles, and small vases—what they call "still life" in English or "silent nature" in Arabic. Why do they say it's silent? If you only knew how much I liked this expression when I first heard it. A speaking nature and a non-speaking nature. Of the two, I loved silent nature. You see, I'm painting my dreams after all these years. My paintings are dreams that flood my waking hours.

After drawing people at Paris cafés for a while, I drew George Bahgoury himself, and I mailed it to *Sabah al-kheir*. Two weeks later, I found my illustration published in the young artists' section, my name below it. Magic and wonder flooded over me—I hadn't expected this twist.

I called for my mother: "Come see my painting!" Her pale face beamed with joy and she kissed me, the tears springing to her eyes. This turn of events gave me more confidence and cemented my sense of specialness. The tears shining in my mother's eyes unconsciously turned my thoughts to my responsibility.

I started looking for my own special subject. I started a fresh sketchbook and wrote on the first page: "Yusuf Tadrus draws from Ghayath al-Din Street." Then I drew the upholsterer, the tinker, Amm Ads the bean seller, and everyone I met. Maybe one day I'd paint from Paris. The notion spurred me on, and the desire to draw seized me, as if I'd reach Paris tomorrow. A fresh sense of life pulsed in my fingers. The pictures didn't look exactly like their subjects, but they were good-natured, with a playfulness and childlike sensibility that came from empathizing with the subjects.

On Ghayath Street, the door and window frames were made of plaster. When pieces fell off, it was material to make small figurines: girls and horses and knights, creatures in the vein of the mulid sugar dolls. I'd scavenge the plaster pieces like they were treasure and sculpt my figures with an old knife and a nail: primitive sculpting tools. I created my world of creatures. One day, I fashioned a small gun. My friends liked it and haggled with me for it. I made more, and they became our favorite toys.

Because of the sculpting and drawing, I had some standing among my childhood comrades in the alley and the nearby streets. They wouldn't play until they'd first passed by my place. When we were in the third year of middle school, they'd stand at the entrance to the alley in the evenings and call for me to come study with them at Sayyid al-Bahiy's house on the corner. We'd go in the back door, from the alley, not the main door on Ghayath al-Din, then cross the vast garden where the plants had shriveled up, and study in the small room in the garden. We'd stay up until the end of the last screening at the cinema and hear the clamor of people leaving, dispersing in the streets. We'd get bored with the room and go sit under the lamppost in the street, studying and talking. When the night began to leave and the morning broke in the distant sky with its pale-blue phantoms, someone would propose praying the dawn prayer at al-Sayyid al-Badawi Mosque.

The streets were still and voices rang out, a translucent fog confirming the coming of the dawn light. When we reached al-Sa'a Square, I'd usually suggest walking in the silence of al-Bursa Street then taking a right on al-Athar Pass. Faint light coming from an open house that had left the entry lamp on; two-wheeled carts resting on the side of the road, their shafts leaning on the ground like weary sleepers; the wooden shop doors shuttered with a slanted iron bar, a brass lock gleaming in the middle; cats crisscrossing the street—the street appeared at odds with the clamor of daytime with the scent of spices and apothecaries and seed shops. By the time we reached the Ahmadi Mosque Square, a silvery glow permeated the light.

Joking, al-Sayyid al-Bahiy would say, "Come on and pray with us."

"Say hi to the crocodile for me," I'd say.

I would wait for them on the marble steps until they came out from the prayer.

At that time, I didn't distinguish a difference in religion from a difference in features, families, and names. People couldn't have the same name or features, and the same went for religion. On Fridays, when we'd climb the wall of Dr. Murqus's house to pick mulberries and play until prayer time, I wanted to go to the Aziz Fahmi Mosque to pray with them. On one of those days, Sayyid al-Bahiy invented a story, the gist being that there was a large fountain in the mosque that held a big crocodile that recognized Christians by their smell and would gobble them up. Every time they went to pray, I'd wait for them, hoping I'd get a chance to see the fountain and the crocodile, just like I wanted to see the creatures that finished the carpets in the weaving workshop.

# Yusuf Tadrus says:

MY FATHER'S A WHOLE OTHER STORY. He thought a lot of himself and would speak his name with pride: Khawaga Tadrus Bushra. But he was ashamed because he couldn't read and write very well, so he took great pains to write his name with care and sophistication. He would sweep the tail of the *a* to encircle the entire name. Maybe because contracts are so important and a man's signature at the bottom of documents is a grave thing, he poured his interest in the written language into signing his name. A name is man's image on official paper, and he should be conscious of this fact. He's got to pay attention. Yes, he would skim the newspapers, but the important thing was that he could write his name with the sophistication befitting a signature.

He was embarrassed by the idea of a stamp or a thumbprint, saying with some uncertainty, "True, my education is modest, but I'm not one of those people who signs with a thumbprint."

When a discussion with his fellow dry bean and seed traders would grow heated, he would stand, leaning his arms on his desk, and say with pride, "Khawaga Tadrus Bushra is not a wrongdoer." Saying that, he'd feel that his name alone was enough to place him beyond reproach for any fault. In those moments, he would pronounce it in dulcet tones, as if he were signing it and looping the tail of the *a* around it.

During the long periods he spent at the shop, he was careful to keep the newspaper spread out in front of him on the desk. He'd look at it, his eyes picking out a word here and there, and beam with self-importance when a trader would come in and find him with the paper open. Then he'd get up from his chair, adjust the collar of his Saidi gallabiya and his headgear—a wool skullcap wrapped in a white scarf—and extend his hand to welcome the guest.

In my childhood, I would go to the shop—he called it "the exchange"—on Fridays after the prayer, to help with the crowds buying lentils, fava beans, and chickpeas, inspecting the bigwigs visiting from the countryside. Mulids and feast days were jam-packed and I had to spend time there. One bark from Khawaga Tadrus would nail you to your spot and turn your limbs to jelly. I'd stand with the workers in the display line until he gave me permission to leave. His shop was his pride and joy because the rural dignitaries trusted him and didn't hesitate to leave their goods with him for safekeeping. But his eyesight started to go and he began submitting himself to Futna, my older sister.

Under the glass on his desk were several newspaper clippings. A family obituary from Upper Egypt, relatives in Alexandria. He never cut his ties with his family. Every year he had to travel to Upper Egypt, the Said, to make deals for dates and seeds and he would revive the bond that should never die with time. Once he showed me an old photo under the desk glass.

"You know who that is?" he asked me.

The photo showed a foreign soldier in military uniform and a short, slim, bareheaded man standing next to him wearing a country-style gallabiya. When I remained silent, he said, "Your father, Tadrus Bushra."

He told me that when people left Alexandria during the Great War, when the Germans were at Alamein—at the gates of Alexandria—he went there to make his fortune, which he used to open the exchange.

Every time he saw me drawing, he'd get angry and say that I had to learn to read and write. I had to study so I wouldn't be a disappointment like my sister Futna's kids. He thought reading and writing, not painting, were the light of life. Drawing was child's play.

It was his experience talking. In Alexandria, during the Great War, he had realized that writing was important when he went looking for work at the English base.

"You're no good for work with us unless you know how to read and write," the soldier told him.

That same day he went to his cousin's in Muharram Bey and spent three full days and nights without sleep trying to learn how to write. He failed. He went back to the base exhausted and told the English soldier what he'd done. Laughing at his naïveté, the man hired him, on condition that he keep up his studies. He hadn't known that learning to read and write was so difficult. Since then, he had revered anyone who could read and write, especially scholars who read complicated books.

The soldier let him work selling scrap from the base, and a few small transactions allowed him to save some money, which at that time was a fortune. The war ended and he returned to Tanta feeling that he had truly become Khawaga Tadrus Bushra, known far and wide.

Sometimes he would fix his gaze on the photo and chew over "the days of youth," thinking he'd accomplished what no one else had. In fact, he hadn't gone to Alexandria by choice, as I later learned from Futna. He went to escape his grief after his son Michel drowned in the Nile during the mulid of the Virgin in Minya, followed soon after by the death of his first wife. A year later, he came to Tanta to live with his uncle, bringing seven-year-old Futna with him. He refused to take her with him to Alexandria. The world's a dangerous place, and she had to stay with his uncle until things settled down. He returned a few years later, opened the shop, and bought a house with all its outlying rooms in the alley where we lived, near Ghayath al-Din Street. All grown up now, Futna became his companion and household manager. When it came time for her to marry, he cried like a child. He couldn't imagine living alone between four walls.

He threw himself into his business and his travels to the countryside to buy crops, as if fleeing his solitude at home. That's when Futna got the idea to marry him off. She knew how stubborn he was, but she knew his weak spot too.

Trying to convince him of the marriage, she told him, "One, she's a light-skinned woman. Two, she's God-fearing. And three, she knows how to read and write."

He lifted his face. "She really knows how to read and write?" he said in a quiet voice. Then he was silent and shifted his gaze upward, and Futna knew he'd agreed.

Khawaga Tadrus married a second time at age forty-five. When I was born, his feelings were different from my mother's. He didn't come near me or speak to me. He treated me oddly. But I know now that his feelings toward me were driven by the fear of death. Futna told me that when he heard me crying at the moment of birth, his face clouded over, as if he were about to face the same pain yet again. He didn't want to experience the infirmity of bone and the fragility of resolve caused by grief. He didn't approach me or call me by name—"Boy," he'd say—turning me over completely to the instruction of the Sitt, the Lady, Umm Yusuf, as he called my mother.

With me, he acted the opposite of what everyone expected. Futna would joke with him: "I told you God wouldn't forget you. He's made it up to you and gave you back His gift."

"Stop with that worthless women's talk," he would respond angrily.

She'd laugh, knowing his quick temper. She was the only one who could claim that she saw into his heart, but because of his steeliness and his skillfulness at concealing his feelings, even she started to believe that he didn't care about her younger brother. That piqued her self-regard: though he was given the son he'd wanted, she would remain the beloved, the daughter of the beloved.

He fortified himself against the tenderness of the heart—that should be left to women—but the anxiety never left him. It was like he knew the capriciousness of the world and didn't believe its sparkle.

And then the day came when they told him, as he was standing at the door of the exchange, that Yusuf had been run over by a truck on al-Nahas Street. That was the day the fog descended over his eyes. The moment he'd feared for so long had come. He heard Sadiq, a worker in the shop, say, "Let's go to the hospital, sir." But he couldn't walk. He sat down on the wooden bench next to the door and said in a voice that puzzled the worker and even himself: "Make sure Umm Yusuf is okay."

The afternoon of that Friday metamorphosed into dusk. Needling him later, they would ask him about Yusuf's boyhood accident—did it happen during the afternoon or at dusk? He would insist that it was dusk and they'd laugh, and he would curse them and say they were cattle who couldn't tell broad daylight from dusk. He wasn't joking. He had absolutely no doubt that the accident occurred at dusk, though it actually happened on a Friday afternoon. He would curse them, saying he saw better than they did, that they were the blind ones.

The fog that settled over my father's eyes was, in his view, fleeting—a brief muddle that would resolve itself soon enough. He waited a long time for the fog to lift, for shapes to be revealed and some of their clarity to return. But it did not happen. To prove to himself and those around him that his eyesight was fine, he would leave the house every morning for the exchange, walking in the fog and stubbornly refusing to rely on anyone, convinced the fog would clear. But one day he felt unsettled. The streets seemed to be shaking and he realized he wouldn't be able to make it alone.

"Stop me a carriage, Umm Yusuf, to take me to the exchange," he said with unpracticed nonchalance.

From that day, Futna began leaving the chickpea stand next to al-Sayyid al-Badawi Mosque and coming to escort my father to the exchange. She'd carry dinner to him in the evening and chat with him about his hard work, telling him he should pack in the business and relax, and because he was nettlesome, he would hold his tongue and then say with a seriousness that would silence her, "Getting greedy, Fatin?"

When he said her given name, she'd know what kind of mood he was in and stop talking.

# Yusuf Tadrus says:

THAT WAS A DIFFICULT DAY that can't be passed over so easily.
You won't understand my tale unless I describe the accident
to you. Listen, the human being is a web of threads. I often
reflect on my life. I arrived bound to a boy drowned in the
Nile years before my birth; to a father who felt inferior to those
who read and write, took pride in himself, and locked up his
feelings in his heart; to a mother who wanted to dedicate herself to the Lord. All of these unseen threads came together to
form your brother Yusuf Tadrus. These invisible threads are
me. They secretly guide me, just like my life was guided by an
invisible fear born the day of the accident and emerging years
later in my paintings.

I wished I could paint the terror of the day of the accident
to rid myself of it, but that's contrived. Terror became my
friend, trifling with me and playing hide-and-seek. Sometimes
it seems that I've rid myself of it, but it's there, undying. I
even discovered it appears in the eyes of the cats I paint. Facing death is important—a person should do it at least once to
understand the meaning of life. Facing death is like the dream
of resurrection. It takes you to the edge and lets you peer into
the abyss.

You know those children's tricycles? On the corner of
Ghayath Street, Amm Rizq would rent them out and take a
deposit to make sure we brought them back in good shape.
That day I rented one and started racing with the boys. The

23

streets were empty then—this was the 1960s. We came out into al-Nahas Street, the cold air buffeting my face. I loved doing tricks, like letting go of the handlebars and raising my hands in the air or putting my fingers in my mouth and letting out our standard whistle. I raised my eyes to the road and saw a monster coming. Don't look at me like that. Really, I saw a monster bearing down on me. You know those old trucks? They had a long nose that looked like a ghoul. I saw the devil in that moment. Finally, the wind started to subside. I wanted to resist the monster, but it pounced on me before I could. I was finished. I died. You can see the scars, this long line on the side of my face, starting at the hairline above my forehead.

I was seven years old. The fractures mended and the long line on my face is no longer noticeable. It became as you see it now, as if it's one of the wrinkles on my forehead. But something in my soul was consumed, or fried, like kids say today.

I'll tell you what I think after all these years. I think the accident blew out some coping center. A kind of fear settled inside me, like part of my flesh, coating my soul in a shiny shell of oil. I smell it, believe me. I smell it whenever something unexpected happens. I smelled it a lot when I'd take the train to teach at the Kafr al-Zayyat School. Painting rescued me from these fears. Look closely at the cats in my paintings and you'll understand the degree of terror I'm talking about.

I smell the scent of fear a lot these days. Whenever I get on the bus and see ever more women with covered faces. Whenever I hear a dog bark. The fear surrounds me, like a mood inseparable from one's features, hand gestures, and tone of voice. You know that tone I use to tell you "Bye-bye, mate"? That's fear: a wretched attempt to get close to people, and false as well because it's a plea, not a real desire for intimacy.

I'll tell you what's even stranger. My eyes were green like my mother's, but now look, they have no definite color. You can't tell if they're green or gray. That gray phantom came with the accident. I *thought* I died, you say. No, I *did* die, and was reborn. I've dreamed often of that moment, and every time I do, I wake up wanting to paint the dream, but I can't. It creeps in and inhabits all my paintings. The monster swallowed me in his maw, and when I returned to life, I was resurrected from the maw of fear. I'm the son of fear. Maybe I'll always be afraid. Don't worry, I've grown accustomed to my fears and befriended them like amusing little pets. I find them teasing me good-naturedly and looking out at me from inside my paintings.

They told me later that my mother was taking a bath. They knocked on the door and told her, "Your son Yusuf's been hit by a car." At that moment, her hair crackled and the roots dried up. She threw on her clothes and ran. After she came back from the hospital, she caught herself in the mirror. Her hair had gone white. As for our old pal Khawaga Tadrus, the fog settled over his eyes, but because of his pride he'd never admit it was the accident that later made him unable to manage his business. Until the day a bailiff showed up to sequester the shop.

The world changed course because of a coincidence. On that day, Futna came running from al-Sayyid al-Badawi Square, her scarf still in her hand. She gave the bailiff five pounds and stopped the seizure. Two days later, she took my father and sat him down at his desk. Then she grabbed the boy Sadiq by the collar and without speaking she head-butted him and cracked open his skull. The blood gushed over the hand that gripped his collar.

Dragging him into the street, she said for all to hear, "You cheat! You son of cheats! You bite the hand that fed you? Not you and not the snake that put you up to it will ever get the exchange!"

The debt was one thousand pounds, at that time an enormous sum. Did you know that a kilo of meat cost fifty piasters at the time? At the lawyer's, she learned of the plot hatched by Sadiq and another trader to take the shop. My father's looped signature was on a promissory note. The next day, she sat on the chair in front of the desk.

"Did you sign a promissory note?" she asked my father.

He raised his head. "Me, sign a promissory note? Never."

"But it's your signature exactly, and your handwriting. I saw the note myself. The spitting image of your handwriting."

Silent, he looked away. He knew he had never signed a promissory note, and it kept eating at his heart. His life was thrown into confusion and he could no longer think. For him, the problem wasn't the thousand pounds. It was how someone could have imitated that signature he'd prided himself on his whole life. It was the first time his self-confidence had taken such a dive. He turned himself over to Fatin that day and let her close the shop and escort him to the chickpea stand on the other side of the square.

Futna sent for me, asking me to take my father home. At first he refused to take my arm, but when I walked next to him, he leaned on my shoulder. It was the first time we were so close. We crossed al-Athar Pass to al-Sa'a Square. He had become so slim and short that I felt he'd shrunk in the years separating the fog's descent on his eyes and the appearance of the promissory note. A few short years had worn him out.

At the square, empty on that summer night, we heard the clamor of moviegoers leaving the last show, their voices loud as we entered Aziz Fahmi Street. I noticed he was mumbling something. Forgetting the small boy leading him, he was talking to himself.

"Just hold tight, Tadrus. You're not one to be broken by a debt of a thousand pounds."

He was leading me now. When I tried to walk on Taha al-Hakim Street, he gripped my shoulder and led me forward, continuing his mumbling. When we reached the alley, he couldn't enter the house.

"Get me a chair, Yusuf, my son," he told me. It was the first time I'd heard him speak my name: Yusuf, my son.

He sat on the chair in front of the house, still whispering to himself, his crisis at its peak. No matter how they tried to persuade him, he wouldn't agree to go back to carrying a seal tied to a woven string in his vest pocket. For him there could be no business without his signature. He began to doubt his ability to carry on with the trade. His end came when his faith in his signature collapsed.

He continued to leave the house every morning, imperious and wanting to rely on himself. The daylight helped him find his way in streets and alleys he knew every inch of. Workers at nearby exchanges would help him open up his shop and sit there. Fatin would come running from the square.

"When are you going to stop this, Khawaga?" Fatin would tell him. "Listen, pack in the business and come work with us—with me and my husband."

He'd answer with his oft-repeated response: "Your husband's greedy. He'd eat up my money and then wipe the bowl clean with me."

In the end, he was compelled to quit his business and do what Fatin urged. He finally submitted to his fate, saying in a low voice, "Futna's right."

# Yusuf Tadrus says:

THE ALLEY WHERE I GREW up is like a courtyard, closed on itself. My father bought it in the late 1940s, a house with some outlying rooms. He used it to store goods, and then he started renting out the rooms to small families. So each room became an independent house, but it preserved the feel of one home. The people of the alley were one family whose center was the house of Khawaga Tadrus. That was the world I was born into. My mother said the women used to spirit me away as a child, and at the end of the day she wouldn't know which house to fetch me from. That's the part of my life I don't know, and what I don't know may have had more of an impact on my constitution than what I know and tell you. There's a warmth and a shadowy longing in my being, but in any case, each of us has his own lost paradise.

In the rooms attached to the house lived several families. Salih al-Naggar, an army enlistee, and his wife from al-Agizi. He was a womanizer and had a library, all of it religious books, and he hung a photo of himself and Sheikh al-Shaarawi facing the door. He sent many letters to the radio, asking the announcer Nadia Salih to visit him and tape an episode for the program *From Someone's Private Library*. Across from his room lived Zinat, the wife of Hassanein the mechanic. She was a beautiful, shapely woman who spent her time in a slip, not caring that people could see her from the window. Salih would chat her up and she'd respond, "Not if you were the last man on earth" or

"Not a chance, you clodhopper." Hagg Ibrahim also lived in the alley with his wife and daughters, as did Umm Samra with her four kids and Umm Bisa with her husband the truck driver.

They lived in the alley as one family. When the crab peddler would enter with his basket on his shoulder, he'd leave with nothing. The women would gather around the catch and take it all. In the afternoon the smell of boiling crab laced with cumin would settle over the alley.

One afternoon, during the summer, Zinat got the idea to use the clothesline strung in the middle of the alley as a volleyball net. Three women gathered and took a plastic ball from a boy and started a volleyball match. Sheer joy filled the place, frivolity, fun, and heartfelt laughter—when I recall the scene, my heart hums. I was sitting on the edge of Umm Bisa's windowsill watching the match, the other women doubled over in laughter in front of the doors.

When we hit puberty, the atmosphere in the alley helped us learn the secrets between men and women without fear or complex. The open life let us experiment with simple, harmless things. Honestly, it's like the alley was lined with an intense sensuality. We observed sexual tensions from their onset, and we'd ask outright for a kiss or a cuddle. Some of us would furtively watch a woman undressing, and at night whispers would reach us from nearby rooms: the demurral, the negotiations, the small gasps, the consoling words after disappointment.

One day I was studying with the boys on the roof when Zinat came up to feed the ducks, wearing just a slip. Aroused, the boy Sayyid Uthman started whispering and biting his lower lip, pointing her out. I was sure she'd noticed us, but she didn't look our way. Then disaster struck: she squatted to set out the food for the ducks, and you could see everything—she wasn't wearing underwear. "Oh my God, she's *trying* to turn us on!" the boy whispered. He started saying her name, sighing and shivering audibly as we laughed. But Zinat paid us no mind. She was talking to the ducks without looking at

30

us. Sayyid Uthman couldn't take it. He went and stood by the chicken coop, pulled out his dick, and started wanking. We laughed at his lack of discipline, especially when Zinat got up to go downstairs and looked at us and smiled.

That environment let us live an almost communal life. The doors were always open and you could enter any door and eat anywhere. In the evening, our living room would fill up with the women, girls, and boys to watch a soap or the program *Songs from the Movies*. There was no television in the alley save the one in the home of Khawaga Tadrus. The children would fall asleep and some of the women would head home, while one would stay with Umm Yusuf to divulge her sadness or fears or ask for advice. My mother would console, soothe cares, and quote bits of wisdom from soaps and films. The television bolstered our household's status in the alley.

The day of the abdication in June 1967 I was young. The whole alley was in the living room, from the youngest child to the oldest men whom we virtually never saw except on holidays, since they left in the early morning and only came back late at night.

The television was in the living room. We couldn't see the screen because of the daylight coming from the stairwell. My father got up and put a blanket on the door, so the rays wouldn't reflect off the screen. He sat there angrily that day. When the president said that he accepted responsibility and was turning the country over to Zakariya Muhiy al-Din, the women wailed. He stood up from the couch and bellowed at them, and then said to Hagg Ibrahim, "What kind of talk is that? Where's he going to go? He's going to leave all these people?"

I didn't understand the horror of it for people until my mother's story about my father. He left the house in a fury that day and went to Shamhut's place, where he drank a pint of gin. At the end of the night he staggered back. That was the only time in his life he ever did that.

My father always felt he owned the alley and was lord of the manor, but he was only home for short spells. Most of his time was spent at the exchange. But when the fog descended on his eyes—and after he closed up shop and went in with Fatin and her husband in the chickpea trade—he started spending lots of time sitting on a wooden chair, resting his chin on his cane.

In the morning he'd sit waiting for Fatin to send one of the workers or her sons to escort him to the display stand. Fatin was even more worried about her father. The streets were no longer safe and cars had multiplied and zoomed up the streets. Accidents were frequent. She had warned us all to take care not to let him walk alone, but the old man's pride had not died. He'd wait silently for a long time until a certain moment came, then the alley residents would look over and find the chair empty. He had gotten up and walked by himself, putting himself in the Lord's hands. He'd cross the streets with deliberation and vigilance, until Fatin would see him coming up Umar Saafan Street. Then she would run to meet him and chide him for not waiting for her to get him.

My father's presence in the alley put a kind of brake on the open life. Even though the man couldn't see well, his sitting in his chair for long periods led the women to seclude themselves a bit. Anyone who saw him like that, staring into space, wouldn't believe he saw the world in shadows. He would sit silently in his place, moving his chair with the sun and recognizing people by voice and smell. His keen attentiveness made people doubt the blindness story. The young men would murmur that he could see but was faking it. He would fix his eyes on a person approaching as if he saw him or her.

In the alley my father became aware of details he hadn't noticed before. He was shocked to learn that Umm Bisa kept company with the jinn and that the boy Tawfiq who lived on the corner was mad and beat his sisters. He smiled with understanding when he realized the appetites Zinat whetted in the neighborhood. He started following the goings-on around him, as if living among us for the first time. Salih al-Naggar took to sitting next to him and joking with him. They would kid around for a long time. Then the conversation gradually turned to religion. Salih imagined he could sway Khawaga Tadrus in matters of religion, until one day he silenced him, saying suddenly, "Salih, son of al-Naggar, you're a charlatan!"

At night, the young guys would stand on the corner, talking and inventing various kinds of fun: who could drink a bottle of soda in one go, who could hit the lamppost with a brick at a certain distance. At that time, the bet involved catching the rats that had proliferated in the alley after the death of one of Zinat's ducks. That was the moment my father's mood soured. He wanted to be out of the house any way he could, for he feared nothing so much as rats.

In the evening, he'd hear Salih and the neighborhood guys hunting rats with a pellet gun. He gave a start with every shot. Their squeals scared him, and he was pleased with the small pops, hoping they'd be decimated. But he hid his feelings and cursed the youths. When he saw one, he'd damn him and his father for having no job and nothing to do.

"Each one of you is as big as an ox," he'd say. "Go get a job. Why don't you go to Port Said and buy some goods to sell?"

His dread of rats remained concealed, though it came out in his anxiety and his feeling that a rotten stench pervaded everything. He started bathing often and asking my mother to dab him with cologne. Then things came to a head.

One day he heard a knock on the door.

"Who is it?" he said quietly.

"Tadrus Bushra," a rough voice said. "A summons from the court."

He bolted off the couch for the door and reached for the lock, guided by habit. His dim eyes saw a huge rat swaying in the air. In a flash, his eyes comprehended the sight and transmitted the requisite terror to his consciousness. He smelled the rotten stench and nearly choked.

Backing away, he cried, "Papa, come quick, oh Papa!" Then he tripped and fell on his back.

Umm Samra came running when she heard the man's shout, cursing Salih and the no-good kids. Entering the living room, she lifted my father to his feet and led him to the couch, smoothing out his clothes and saying, "It's okay, brother, God's name protects you."

He later learned that Salih and the kids had devised a trick for him. They hung from a fishing line one of the rats they'd caught, and one of them had gone to the roof and dangled the rat in front of the door while another knocked. That night he regained his strength and went out with the gnarled cane, intending to crack open Salih's gourd. When the neighbors intervened, he insisted that Salih leave the house. He had to pack up his things and go. The people's sentence for Salih was that he not sleep at home for several days, until they could calm Khawaga down. A few days later, Salih returned with Hagg Ibrahim.

"I'll kiss your hands and feet, Papa Tadrus. Please forgive me!" he said with true contrition.

That was enough for my father to bark, "Get out of my sight, I don't want to see your face."

# Yusuf Tadrus says:

I LEARNED TO PAINT IN the studio of Hazim al-Shirbini in the Palace of Culture on al-Bahr Street, the old building demolished in the late 1970s where the Gharbiya Bank now stands. On the first floor was a library, a little dark because the large windows were blocked by bookcases; the rest of the rooms were filled with employees. On the second floor there was a broad hall with a piano. Any time you'd enter you'd find Amm Farid, the music teacher, playing chess. The spacious painting studio was on the right, with a wooden floor and a balcony across from the door. Light flooded the place.

We sat in front of the easels for the first time to paint in oils, we three boys who had won the painting contest sponsored by the Palace of Culture: Karim al-Burai, Muhammad Tawfiq, and Yusuf Tadrus.

We started lessons in the summer, training in pencil, then doing charcoal sketches. I was the most nervous of them, maybe the most interested. Muhammad Tawfiq was the son of a civil servant in the tax authority who was preparing himself to be a painter. Karim al-Burai was from a merchant family. Slim, tall, and carefree, he liked to paint as a kind of entertainment, to test himself. As for me, it was like a window of light had opened. I'd finally left the alley and begun another journey.

It seems like it happened so long ago, like the world was new. It was quiet and the streets were so empty you could hear the clop of the hooves of horses pulling carriages. There weren't many taxis—life hadn't yet been drowned out by the racket. Sometimes I'm shocked by how my life took shape out of such a gelatinous mass. I remember us sitting there, doing charcoal sketches. The studio in the Palace of Culture created something precious: deliverance from the muck of the neighborhood and the preoccupations of the alley. My passions found their vessel.

The first day, Hazim al-Shirbini stood in the middle of the room. His long hair reached the wide, starched collar of his shirt, and the top buttons were open, showing some stray hairs. He talked about mass and space, perspective and lines in an interesting way, holding a piece of paper he'd use to quickly illustrate what he was saying. He spoke cheerfully and airily, like he was chatting up a girl. He'd recently graduated from the College of Arts in Cairo and had been appointed to the Palace of Culture, so he was excited about teaching painting. He actually helped to foster a different air in the city. A world of joy blossomed when I began drawing sketches under his tutelage. I was on the threshold of the dream.

The first time painting with oils was nerve-racking, maybe frightening. That day Hazim put a tablecloth and a brown bottle on a small table and asked us to paint them. The anticipation and excitement I experienced that day heightened my sense of light, summoning all my past observations of it and making the first attempt at oil painting more difficult. It was a summer afternoon, and the sun bathed the entire balcony.

At first I couldn't concentrate, unsure about where to begin. I avoided it by contemplating the light on the balcony. I observed the shadows instead of the light—shadow is light from the other side. The light of the summer sun left heavy shadows of the balcony ironwork and exposed the roughness of the rust. I was afraid. How could I represent that? I put down the brush and went to stand on the balcony. I watched Hazim standing in the hall, talking amiably to a new employee while Amm Farid was lost in a chess match. I looked down from the balcony. There was a dried-up tree, its limbs twisting in every direction,

36

making an intricate horizontal cross-section. Copper-colored fruit like dark seeds protruded from the sides of some limbs. I followed the limbs, their different thicknesses, their rising and falling, the bends and intersections. I was absorbed in observation until Hazim called me from the hall.

"What is it? What's wrong?"

I was unsettled as I faced serious painting for the first time. I returned to my place in front of the easel. Now I had to complete the picture however I could. Listen, I was worried about my self-image at that early date, scared I wouldn't be up to the picture of myself I'd formed, or that the story of my birth had formed. Mary Labib was present and helped me.

"Paint," she whispered. "Don't be afraid, just paint."

With Mary's voice spurring me on, I painted with speed and force. I represented the bottle, the tablecloth, part of the wooden table, and part of the glass of the balcony door.

The painting was wanting in my view, although Hazim praised it above those of my peers. He said it showed a refined sense of light and shadow, but proficiency required long practice and a painstaking study of light and shadow. It was praise, but it underscored my sense of inferiority, and on my way home I started thinking again of the light.

I remember the scene as I walked amid the tumult of Saad al-Din Street that day. I observed the tremor in the light when a boy on a bike rushed past with a tray of bread on his head. I noted the contrast left by the light reflected on walls and the faces of peddlers. I saw the faint shadow on faces and said to myself: Could I paint that? Where would I get the patience to study and understand all these distinctions when I loved fun and girls and running after whatever caught my fancy?

I was despondent that day, even though my painting was the best one. See? I've had a complex since day one—the neurotic reveals himself at the outset. Instead of being happy that day because I'd painted in oils for the first time, I was thinking about what I lacked.

The studio at the Palace of Culture became a spot of light. I was in the first year of high school, at the beginning of adolescence, getting to know myself and the world. Every day I'd escape the alley and go to the Palace of Culture, regardless of the schedule Hazim had set for us. He was sympathetic, actually. He sensed my need to paint and never asked me why I came at unscheduled times. He left the oils for me to paint with, and I spent days determinedly painting the same bottle, as if it held something alien I needed to grasp. Under my constant scrutiny, it turned into a feminine body. Strips of light slipped into her and formed various shapes in her interior. Ironically, the painting became worse the more I stared at the bottle, until the day when Hazim said, "Enough, Yusuf. The bottle's bewitched you; you'll never paint it well. Paint something else, and go back to it later."

I was sad he didn't let me complete the experiment, but he knew better.

There was another minor incident in that period that had an important influence. Let me tell you about it. One day, I was going up to the second floor of the Palace of Culture and I heard the sound of the piano. It was the first time I'd seen Amm Farid get up from the chessboard and sit on the oval black seat and start to play. Hazim was standing at the studio door, and women employees at the palace were sitting scattered around the hall. Silence enveloped the place. I stood at the door, unable to enter. Amm Farid was playing a piece I thought I'd heard before, maybe in the score of an old film. I don't know, but the feeling captivated me from the first instant. The melodies flowed and formed a feeling like light. I started listening to the music, giving full rein to my imagination. The slow melodies created a space in which dried leaves fell from a tree like the lone tree below the balcony, and the leaves drifted in the never-ending space between the tree limbs and the ground, fluttering, swaying, and shifting.

In truth, I wasn't hearing a piece of music—I was watching a visual experience. That day, for the first time, I understood the concept of creativity.

I was touched by the feelings the music left in my being and told myself I wanted to paint pictures that had the same impact. How could I do that? The question dogged me for a long time without an answer. From that early date, I chose the most difficult point against which to measure myself, without regard for my modest skills. Every painting I do brings to mind my feeling about that piece. I ask myself: Will this painting leave someone with the feeling Amm Farid's music left in me?

At the end of the summer, Hazim al-Shirbini introduced us to the Ankh Society, a group of his friends who met in Hussein Said's house on al-Alfi Street. A new door to knowledge and self-understanding opened before me. There I discovered a different kind of light. The group was made up of Hazim, Hussein Said (the owner of the place), Bilal al-Sheikh, and Mahmoud Qandil, a morose young man with a bristly mustache. He was a communist, and once he started talking, he didn't stop.

The most prominent of them was Bilal al-Sheikh. He'd studied at the College of Fine Arts in Alexandria with Seif Wanli and worked as an art teacher for the education department. He was enthusiastic and thought the arts were the foundation of progress. That was in the summer of 1977, the beginning of the inflation that nipped away at people's wages, the beginning of the traffic and collapse of services.

In our first gatherings, we read the *Manifesto of May 30*, which Bilal had written in 1968. That nine years had elapsed since the penning of the manifesto turned it into a sort of gospel for me, a youth of seventeen who loved absolutes. That you could read a paper written nine years ago when you were a boy playing in the street or hanging off the back of the street-washing truck—it was like you were perusing history.

The manifesto was poetic and utopian and spoke to a person's desire for perfection. Maybe it's *because* it was unworkable that it was so attractive.

I distanced myself from the alley and lived in that unsullied world in Hussein Said's room, embracing the manifesto like a new religion. Despite the surging in my body, my fascination with girls, and collecting the contributions for my mother, the Thursday meeting of the Ankh Society became the most important event in my life. The manifesto was a project for living, for a different life than the one I lived in our house, one that called on you to make "your eye a sun, your ear a sun, and your spirit a sun." The first night after Bilal read out the manifesto for us, I didn't sleep. My tendency to elevate ordinary events to the exemplary is one neurosis I still haven't shaken.

Hussein was smitten by broadcasting. The emergence of the cassette player at that time enabled him to turn the manifesto into a radio piece set to Wagner. He had a melodious voice and thought himself a radio announcer who hadn't yet had his chance. With its high-flown oratory and epic sensibility, the manifesto was like one of those speeches of Abd al-Nasser's we'd begun to miss.

Years later, I was embarrassed by my callowness and took to mocking the Ankh Society and the customs of those nights, when we'd read poetry, listen to music, and contemplate paintings. But trust me, I mocked them in my impotence and failure. Mockery is the tool of the impotent. I mocked them to tell myself I'd grown up and was past that phase. But really, is that true? Isn't my whole life a childish frivolity, evidenced by the fact that I'm still attached to painting so late in life despite few successes, a handful of exhibits, and some individual acquisitions? The more I think of it, I find the teachings of the Ankh Society are the only pure things I tried to embody. Maybe that's the cause of my failure, and also of the modest success of some of my paintings.

There's another way of looking at it. The members of the Ankh Society looked down on people and were deeply insular. Much later, when I noticed this insularity and condescension in myself, I knew it was largely an attempt to endow the self with some worth. This condescension isn't only for arrogant artists of my ilk, but for all figures who set themselves above others, from all religions. The wellspring is this: in this country, you have to carry something sacrosanct in your soul to find your missing value, to cultivate your spirit with some worth above and beyond the neglect by society and the authorities. You'll find this trace of condescension and insularity among members of Islamist groups, monks, and anyone who belongs to the sacred in some way. The only people who escape it are those who instinctively realize that they're just grains of sand, simple ephemeral creatures who pass over the earth like a cloud's shadow. That's a place reached only by the great Sufis and monks and inspired souls. As for all the others, you'll find them perplexed, like your brother Yusuf Tadrus.

Like I said, I was as passionate about the manifesto as if I'd written it. The lovely poetry pervaded me, urging me to make my eyes a sun and my spirit a sun. Since it coincidentally used the metaphor of the sun, it touched the deepest part of my psyche. I began searching for ways to do it: practicing painting and listening to music, reading and deliberating, resisting the seductions that consume energy and time. See? The way of Sufis and monks. Elevating oneself above human life is complicated and baffling, but exciting for a youth of seventeen about to sit for the matriculation exams. One who wants a bit of an escape from the fully corporeal life in his neighborhood. A confused, frightened person who wants a whiff of the absolute.

When school started, it became hard to go to the Palace of Culture. I started the austere year of the matriculation exam, the first person in Khawaga Tadrus's family to make it to the exam. Imagine, the fear of death that accompanied my life was cast outward as a great joy when I was studying that year.

"Yusuf's prepping for the exam," my mother would say from the threshold at Umm Bisa and Hassanein's house. An innocent, ironic smile appeared on my father's face, as if he'd outsmarted the Lord and Yusuf had lived despite the death of his brother and the car accident. When I'd go out on Thursday with my ironed shirt, bell-bottom pants, and platform shoes, my mother's face would cloud over, as she worried that the Ankh Society nights would take me away from studying. The exam was the door that would lead Yusuf to another station. It would save him from the alley. But she knew that stopping me was impossible.

"Take care of yourself, brother," she'd say, allaying her fears. She called me "brother," maybe to revive the secret bond between us on our wanderings in the city to collect the contributions, the feeling underlying the story of my birth. Or maybe to surreptitiously bolster that greatness in my being. Forgive me: I'm trying to understand, but it's hard. Retrieving life at a remove is a difficult thing.

Despite the strain of that period because of my family's focus on the exam, the experience of painting the bottle on the tablecloth in the Palace of Culture abided. I'd escape studying by examining what the experience had left in me. I think the idea that light is the origin of things started then and put down roots. Light is the liquid spirit behind things, the intangible phantom essence. At root, anything can hold a slip of light, a secret spirit. Everything can turn into light.

Vague and distant, these thoughts loomed, naïve and unable to take shape in the mind of a seventeen-year-old boy awash in fears and confusion. It was a difficult task. I'd realized that painting meant you could capture the hidden spirit of the bottle, the vase, and the tablecloth, but how do you acquire the eye to perceive the liquid spirit of inanimate things? Fingers capable of conveying that spirit? How could you grasp a liquid thing like light coursing within everything? Difficult.

I started dodging my studies and spent nights practicing to perfect the lines of the bean pot, or a small plate, or the chair my father sat on, behind the door. I struggled hard and long, but the ideal was so high, beyond my capabilities. I was stubborn like my father.

The next day, I'd say I could paint the water jug in Umm Bisa's window. I could paint my mother's concentration as she chopped the mulukhiya. It was a senseless struggle, because my natural abilities were ordinary. But what can I say? The idea that I was destined for something big lurked beneath every action, deluding me that I could create this thing, that I could reach the liquid spirit underneath things.

The pace of the work I'd assigned myself picked up. I had to study, and I had to practice painting to get into the College of Fine Arts to study with Seif Wanli. The city attracted me and sparked a vague glimmer in my imagination like the glimmer of the phrase "George Bahgoury paints from Paris."

I lived on the margins of my family's life. My father would return at night and when he'd see me, he'd ask, "You still awake?"

"I'm studying," I'd say nervously, hiding my drawing paper.

He'd nod like he understood and believed the lie. At the same time, his gestures and unexpected questions suggested he knew what I was doing.

"I want to see you at college so I can die happy," he said one day.

It was a decisive night in March. I put away the drawings and focused on studying until the end of the year.

# Yusuf Tadrus says:

I SPENT ONE YEAR IN Alexandria. My mother was nervous and happy and calling relatives who lived in Alexandria to tell them that Yusuf was coming to study at the College of Fine Arts. She introduced me to Rida Boulos, a scion of a family long in the leather trade. He was in his third year of studying architecture and lived in an apartment in Sidi Bishr. We agreed I'd live with him. I was anxious that summer, frightened of my mother's overwhelming desire to get me away from the life of the alley.

My relationship with Rida Boulos eased the air somewhat and, perhaps for the first time, set the idealistic life of the Ankh Society against another way of living. Rida's presence that summer gave me the vigor I needed. Despite his seriousness, he was preoccupied with girls like we were. We went out often, to weddings and parties. I'd boast about how girls were attracted to me, and he'd look at me with childish glee and say, "You lucky dog, Yusuf." But I feared that attachment and avoided it. I tried to show it didn't matter to me. We'd categorize the girls together: that one was like a princess, this one a saint. This other one was like the wicked witch, and that one might bring you to ruin and go through your pockets every night.

Rida was cheerful and outgoing, and wore his religion lightly. His heart wasn't home to vague fears and anxious questions. He felt comfortable in the world and easily did things I thought required a slew of preparations. He'd pack a big suitcase and a tent and go to Sidi Abd al-Rahman alone to stay in the desert a few days. He'd do his share of work for his family. He'd travel to Upper Egypt. He went to Paris twice.

His way of acting and talking, his perpetual urgency, and his feeling that he shouldn't waste one second stood in contrast to the lackadaisical life in the alley, which revolved around managing everyday affairs. And it was also obviously different from the philosophers of the Ankh Society. He'd laugh when I'd tell him about the society's sessions every Thursday.

"They're not living on this earth," he'd say. "Life isn't talk; it's action, movement."

He studied architecture and painted, and wanted to learn to play the lute. I introduced him to Amm Farid. I wondered how he could find the time amid his work to learn to play the lute.

He laughed. "I'll keep at it until circumstances intrude and stop me," he said. "At least I'll have gotten something out of it to help me listen better."

He had his own ideas, not formed from books but created from his own experiences and thoughts.

It was the first time the secretive salon and closed world of the Ankh Society was shaken. The contradiction added to my angst. I spoke with Bilal about it one day, and he said confidently that my friend was superficial, flaky, and didn't live the authentic life—he lived by mainstream thought, not his own personal thought. The authentic life was something else. This idea of the "authentic" life preoccupied me. What was it and how could one live it? There was no manual. The plan they'd drawn up for it started to show cracks when confronted by the other worlds that opened before me.

That summer the covert war began between my mother and older sister. Futna was my father's true mistress. She took care of everything, knew all the expenses, and amassed wealth she kept far from him and us. My mother's aspirations began to run up against the parsimony with which Futna managed life. My moving to Alexandria and the expense of the College of Fine Arts sparked long discussions. Khawaga Tadrus didn't get involved in them, leaving the conflict between the two women to work itself out.

Futna would reel off the costs of residency, living expenses, clothes, and college needs: that was a lot for an old man whose sight had gone. My mother would minimize things, saying she'd help with expenses from the stipend she got from the Holy Bible Association. She was fervent, and the conflict was settled.

On the eve of my travel to Alexandria my fears began. Rida had gone before me to take care of some business, and when I reached the Sidi Gaber station at night, the expanse of the square scared me. I'd visited Alexandria several times with my mother, and now I was standing at the station gate, feeling so small in that sweeping place. I took the tram and reached the apartment, and then I spent the night walking along the Corniche, unable to sleep. For the first time in my life, I was far away from the bosom, from the alley, from my father's throat-clearing and my mother's mumbled prayers. I was a child being weaned. Is that how to understand the pain of that year? Maybe there was something else I didn't realize. Maybe I didn't want that spaciousness and freedom.

In the first days at college, the fear grew. I had to push through the days.

"What is it, Yusuf? Are you made of wood?" Rida would tease.

But he misspoke—I was made of clay. The cause of my yearning for light was my earthy nature. I was from the alley, and I loved to play in that muddy water. I stayed up at night practicing painting fingers, faces, and feet. I'd study the anatomy of the skull, the shape of the eye, the details of neck muscles. Sometimes I'd long to paint something cheerful. I'd set up the easel and prepare the oils and start painting an ashtray on a small table.

I couldn't paint anything properly. The proportions escaped me, as if my training had been poured into a void.

When trying to place mass in a space, an essential skill for anyone who wants to be a painter, I felt like a blind man.

Rida Boulos liked some of the paintings and said I'd be an artist. Sometimes he'd set up his own easel and paint a teapot or chair with me, or an empty bottle. One day we painted three onions against the lead-gray wall of the room. I was worked up that day. I painted the three onions on a green tablecloth against a fire-red background. The painting captured the details faithfully but had a surrealist feel to it. Rida looked at it.

"I'm giving up painting, Yusuf," he said.

And from that day, or maybe a little afterward, he no longer painted, like he'd made a decision. Despite his encouragement, I couldn't continue. I saw the flaws more than my abilities.

Rida helped me my whole life. At that early stage of our acquaintance, he was bewildered by my nature and my neuroses. He'd say I needed to smash everything and paint whatever I wanted, whatever gave me pleasure, whatever I gravitated toward. I thought he was naïve—Bilal had equipped me with the proper geometric calculations for every good painting, and we'd often applied them to the work of the great artists, from the classical arts down to Egyptian artists. I was miserable because I couldn't free myself of the manual I had brought with me from Tanta—of the special formula for evaluating artistic paintings—and I started to believe I wouldn't be able to paint as long as I was incapable of creating the equilibrium and correct proportions that Bilal al-Sheikh had prescribed.

With time, I discovered that Alexandria was vaster than I'd imagined. Every day it expanded more and I grew smaller, until I imagined I'd vanish. Midyear, the problems between my mother and sister started because of my school expenses. The college was far beyond my family's capacity, and my own psychological capacity. You need living expenses and clothes and other things. Rida Boulos's sympathy confused me and made me feel indebted and paralyzed. I couldn't bear it any more, and the situation became more difficult when I discovered Lamiya's attraction to me.

One day Fatin sent a message with Rida. He seemed embarrassed when he gave it to me. He was prepared to help me in any way, but he was duty bound to give me the message first. He said Fatin had visited him suddenly at home and had spoken to him about my family's circumstances. She told him my father was blind and couldn't shoulder this burden for five years. It would be better, she said, if Yusuf returned to Tanta and helped with the business. He could study at any college there and it wouldn't cost so much.

That excuse was enough for me to perceive that I wouldn't stay in Alexandria. Then the long winter days set in and I found myself blindly drawn to Lamiya. You know Raphael's paintings? Lamiya was one of Raphael's women, an angel come down to earth. She would stay by my side from the moment I set foot in the college to the end of the day. She'd help me, with that ethereal quality of hers that was so unsuited to me. I'd grown up in an alley. I knew carnal desires. I'd come from a coarse world suffused with the intimation of sexuality, with flirtatious banter and caresses everywhere. I couldn't handle such proximity to the sublime. And then she was from a very wealthy family. I know myself and I know my family—there was no way.

I tired of that intolerable existence. I feared I'd lose my already precarious balance and find I'd done something disastrous. One day I'd found myself kissing her in the middle of the studio.

I felt I was on the verge of disaster whenever we were alone anywhere, even in the college halls. One day I stayed late in the studio. I looked around and found myself alone with Lamiya. I made a hasty exit, leaving her there to ready her supplies with the same ethereal refinement with which she did everything else.

Like I said, the place was bigger than me. I'd known it from the first moment, but hadn't immediately recognized it. When I recall how I stood at the gate of the Sidi Gaber station on my first night in Alexandria, I know my feelings told me the truth. That night I saw myself small in that place. The cars seemed to pass farther in the distance than normal, the buildings were taller than normal, sizes bigger than they really were, and I was smaller than my true size. The cold air had an impersonal, salty smell. Even the blue tram swayed in a stately manner as it entered the station.

Years later, I understood the meaning of my feelings. I was coming from the alley, and my size in the alley was right for my status. Things were close by, within arm's reach, and I was virtually surrounded with attention. The alley was like a womb—I had an organic link to it. When I stood at the gate of the Sidi Gaber station, it was a birth I couldn't bear, so I returned to the warmth of the womb.

These explanations came after the fact as an attempt to silence the anxiety and my feeling that I'd made a mistake by wasting the chance to study at the College of Fine Arts.

In April, I decided to return to Tanta. Rida Boulos was agitated that day.

"You're losing out," he said, angry and serious. "Trust me, you're losing out."

"I don't know," I told him. "Maybe it's for the best."

We remained in contact and would meet whenever he returned from Alexandria, but he was sad. He seemed to honestly believe he was responsible for me.

It was a victory for my sister. Two days after I arrived, my mother came down with a severe cold, then a high fever. I went to the pharmacy on Ghayath Street to buy medicine. I met Dr. Hani, an acquaintance of hers, and he asked about her. I described her condition.

"It could be something other than a cold," he said. "Let me take a look."

He came with me to the house. When he entered her room, she looked at me in reproach, because I'd brought in a stranger while she was sick. He didn't examine her. He said hello and put his palm on her forehead.

"Take her to the fever hospital quickly and I'll catch up with you there," he said.

At the hospital, Dr. Hani found she had typhoid.

"Your mother's a good woman and you were about to lose her," he said.

In the ghostly air of the fever hospital, she looked at me with blame, asking silently why I'd returned from Alexandria. Her silence and melancholy settled in my depths—not because of my failure to complete an arts education, but mostly because of her defeat by my big sister.

The time in the hospital deepened the private bond between us. We were alone in a long ward, among peasant women ailing from different kinds of fevers, surrounded by an unending solitude.

Those three days stretched out in a dark area of my depths. We were alone in the universe, and her hopes that I would turn out to be something were lost. She grieved because I had been the equivalent of giving herself to the Lord; she had only abandoned that path to give birth to Yusuf. I hadn't imagined my return from the arts college would have such a traumatic effect on her.

She had an illuminated area of her soul that got her through those moments. A little later, she started explaining my return from Alexandria in a way that enabled her to preserve her image of me: Yusuf was sacrificing his future to put an end to my problems with his sister. He was helping me live. He only came back from Alexandria to stop the quarreling and humiliation over his expenses. Yusuf didn't want to burden me beyond my capacity.

That was how she construed it, and she began to accept my presence in the alley.

But things didn't stop there. The nagging set in: it's not right for Yusuf to sit around idly in the alley watching the women all day. His father's blind; he's got to help with the work. My older sister set this poison loose in my father's mind.

He asked me to escort him to work every day, his hand grasping my shoulder, silent most of the time. A barrier grew up between him and me in that period, an invisible barrier that kept me from any sympathy for him. I'd stay by his side all day and sometimes I'd find I'd left the display line without a word and gone, walking in the streets aimlessly. I wouldn't go home until after midnight.

Those days were bland, tasteless and formless. My mother's anxiety ballooned when they told her Yusuf had gone off his rocker and would spend a full day without saying a word.

In this wilderness, she took action. She called her relatives and used her connections with someone to get me a job teaching art classes at a private school, as if she intuited the link between the creation of pictures and me. I worked at the school throughout my studies. The free time offered by the College of Humanities allowed me to work, and so I stopped going to the chickpea stand and left behind the world of my father and sister.

At that time I was afflicted with self-loathing because I hadn't been able to live in Alexandria, as if there were something ruined in me, a lack of some sort. How could I refuse the open life and smooth roads? Getting to know major artists? How could I so easily squander all that? How could I be an artist if I couldn't bear life away from my family? I was utterly lost and didn't know where life was taking me. Even my relationships with my pupils at school were bad. I was standoffish and viewed the children with hostility. Though I often thought of Mary Labib and her love, it wasn't enough to improve my mood.

My work at the school put me up close to the girls, to the intimacy and gaiety of their lives, their small tales, and their dreams of finding a husband. It also allowed me some dalliances, not all of which were innocent. Urges would suddenly erupt and you'd find yourself in a fervor you couldn't easily escape. I was infatuated with Nabila with the dimples, Theresa with the budding chest, and Mary and Mona. Sometimes the joking would turn into a brief escapade in a courtyard or next to an apartment door. I wasn't alarmed by the idea of sin like my colleagues at the school. I was drawn to happy-go-lucky girls unfazed by such lapses. They were engaging in a little trivial fun, and we agreed it wouldn't transgress the rights of any future husband.

I loved the fun of this period. Once Theresa told me, "You're a vagabond, Yusuf, and whoever lives with you won't be happy." Angrily, I asked her which fortuneteller had taught her to see into the future.

"What? Did I upset you?" she teased, then said, simultaneously serious and playful, "To tell you the truth, I've considered you and concluded you'll wear my heart out."

"Look, don't tell me that to my face," I joked. "Let me live with the illusion."

We laughed.

Because of the ordinariness of these dalliances, I took a cynical view of the seriousness with which my peers at college approached them—it was all love stories and destiny like they were modeling their lives on an Abd al-Halim Hafez song. Some of them were tortured by it and others became so entangled in relationships it became difficult to extricate themselves. My experience was just ordinary, despite the gravity of it in religious terms.

What can I do? This sensitivity to the love of girls had perhaps been formed over years of living in the alley, observing women, and sensing the ease with which people touched each other; how their relationships evolved and they fell into minor escapades that weren't life-destroying. This sense helped me enjoy these games and softened the austerity of those days. I even felt I'd settle down here. I'd graduate, work as a teacher, and marry one of those girls. But without her dreams. We'd agree to leave her dreams at the apartment door. I'd live an ordinary life.

This plan suited the troubled Yusuf Tadrus, he who carried a heavy load he couldn't then see, placed on his shoulder by a kind woman who'd wanted to give herself over to the Lord.

Because of relationships with coworkers at the school, I started going to church regularly. One day a relative of Theresa said, "Yusuf, you used to paint, right? Paint me."

I looked at her as if I were remembering myself.

"One second," I said. I left the church, bought a ream of paper and a charcoal pencil, and returned. I stood there drawing the girl with swift, happy strokes, a few touches, and light shading until there she was, smiling at me from inside the portrait. Theresa grabbed it and showed it to the other girls, who stood amazed at the precision of the features and the speed with which I'd drawn it.

"Should I take it?" the girl said flirtatiously, holding the portrait.

"Take it," I said immediately, and then laughed. "You want the pencil, too?"

I stood there not knowing what to do. I wanted to draw anything. Everything around me called out to me to paint it. I left the church and went straight home. I set up a place to paint on the roof and started work that very day. Everything I'd penned up during my fear in Alexandria burst forth. I was painting anything around me: the chicken coop, the way the rooster and hens moved. I painted the distant balconies and Amm Said the ironer and the alleyway entrance. Little by little, the obsession with painting arrived like a lifeline. I didn't remember anything I'd learned. I just wanted to put features and the spirit of things on paper.

# Yusuf Tadrus says:

I GOT MANY REQUESTS FOR portraits. It started as a joke, as I told you, but it quickly took on a life of its own and ended up taking up all my attention until I graduated from college. A fertile period during which I really learned. Looking back on my story now, I know that was when I learned the meaning of painting—not the techniques of it, but the meaning. What it is. I was on my own, with little experience and a spirit that longed to step out of its straitjacket. I threw myself into portraiture, a difficult mission. I'm baffled now when I remember how blithely I approached it. If it weren't for Theresa's relative joking at church, it wouldn't have happened. Do you think a person's life is like a game of chess, and if you make one false move, the game is lost? Or is there some hidden spirit in everyone that pursues every path to reach its fate?

When I look over my life, I often think: What if that step hadn't been taken? I try to count the thwarted destinies. I was ultimately convinced of the second notion: every person has a spirit that leads him, an interior sense guiding his path to its end. If the path is blocked here, the impulse persists, waiting for a suitable moment to resume the journey. I have no proof of this, and I know you don't believe in such supernatural mysteries. You think every person's life is what he makes of it and that he creates his own happiness or misery. He can even cope with and rewrite the conditions that shaped his life before he was born. I know, and I know you think the basis of this view of mine is the same as that underlying the idea of the "preserved tablet": predestination. I don't care. This is what remains to me now.

The breakthrough took place on a cheery Sunday evening in the church courtyard, and that whole phase was imprinted with that feeling. If portraiture had taken on the somber gravity of the teachings of the Ankh Society or the academic traditions of the College of Fine Arts, it would have failed. This is support for my argument that destiny was biding its time, out of view, until it could reach its end.

The art of representation is the greatest of the arts. It's the art of creation. Life is exterior manifestation, and representation embodies this exterior and endows it with a character and mood. It lets us contemplate and experience it outside of time. I learned that everything longs to assume concrete form in some consciousness. Even inanimate things yearn for it. They realize the purpose of their existence when they take concrete form.

I learned how to paint portraits by doing them and became familiar with the difficulties inherent in portraiture, sometimes eased by passion. Think about it awhile and you'll see. Facial features aren't fixed like we think they are. Like time, the face is ever changing. Each of us has specific features, but the uninterrupted parade of expressions gives features a different flavor at every instant. We know the features of our friends and relatives as the backdrop for their expressions. This fluidity of spirit behind the features is what you have to capture. You have to convey the spirit of the person in an ephemeral moment, from one particular perspective, amid the dozens of points of light scattered across the face. It's like you're in a maze, not only because of the precise geometry, but because of the fleeting impressions whirling in your mind. You discover the face as you're painting it. The white collar under that brown sweater resembles a priest's collar. The angularity of that nose reminds you of Dr. Bula, the Armenian doctor who died alone in his apartment. Look at those owlish eyes, and those lips, utterly feminine and beguiling. That budding breast contains a potency beyond anyone's capacity. The vitality in that untamed wildness is the equivalent of an atomic blast. This skin has an enchanting gleam. Oh, if she would let me paint her nude—will she?

The people sitting for you are nervous because of the silence and the probing of their faces. It's like someone's peering into their depths and rifling through their secrets. The scrutiny is unnerving. The eyes emit beams, not all of which wish to express the person's features. They have complicated, confused desires. Who can separate the scrutiny of features from searching them? Ultimately, I can't deny that the urge to grasp the lines of the face is married to a kind of totemic sorcery, an attempt to act upon the person sitting before you. Believe me, there's some connection to sorcery. I fell in love with nearly everyone I painted. Some of them spurned and hated me. The sessions painting girls were particularly tense, as if during the painting we'd discover that special thing that made us click. Maybe that's the secret of attraction. When the girl gets to know you and finds you've created her on paper and know her secret, she has to love you. Oh, what if I could paint her nude!

I made that offer to several girls, but only Theresa agreed. She was bold, but it turned out otherwise. On Sunday evening, I went to her aunt's house carrying my materials, excited and expectant. They were all at church. Theresa opened the parlor for me, and we sat talking. I asked her to take off her clothes, but she refused, saying she wouldn't honor the agreement. She'd thought about it and gotten cold feet. I tried to allay her fears. I told her I'd paint the portrait there and leave it for her, if she were afraid I'd spread it around. I told her she needn't be frightened of me. Anyway, she'd already made up her mind and didn't consider me a potential husband. She started to slowly remove her clothes. When her breasts appeared, I dropped what was in my hands and went to her.

She embraced me and I kissed her, but in the end she refused to let me paint her nude, and the dream evaporated.

Getting naked is difficult. This objectivity about the body still isn't common among us, and neither she nor I were prepared for it. I don't know if that was good or bad, but I know that our perception of the body remains very personal and private. To be honest, I tend to think it's something precious we should preserve. Think of Mahmoud Said's women, those Nubian servants—it's sad. Yes, he managed to create that rugged, vital energy he loved, but they were maids. It's hard. Even now, I feel my experience is lacking. It's complicated and I won't be able to talk about it.

Not one of the conservative girls of Tanta let me paint her nude. Some of them even ran into trouble because of the portrait. That was a long time ago. A girl's picture was part of her and she had to keep it out of the hands of young men. If it got around among strangers, it was a scandal. That era was the beginning of the fearlessness and freedom. Maybe also the beginning of the closed-mindedness, I'm not exactly sure. There was a time in the late 1970s and early 1980s that was promising. It was forward-looking and had a youthful feel, like Munir's song about unbuttoning your shirt to the breeze and hopes. There was the Hani Shenouda band, and the Ammar al-Shari'i band—things were bubbling with boldness and a desire to step out. That's when I painted the portraits.

I painted some girls because they were relatives, acquaintances, or flirts. Others I painted in secret in exchange for a kiss and a caress. Some of them were reckless about it, as if they didn't care if their portrait made the rounds.

When a girl allows you to paint her, it means she agrees to let you touch and contemplate her. That was the fun, enjoyable part, but that's not all there was. My name as a painter spread and I started getting requests to paint housewives and middle-aged men. If I had any business sense, I'd be a famous painter now making money off the profession.

I painted elderly women, and mothers came to me to do oil paintings of children who'd died young. I blew up small snapshots of young men who'd traveled and left the town for good. That was at my mother's urging—she couldn't stand the grief of mothers. I summoned spirits and immortalized the ephemeral, and the experience took a toll on my spirit.

Probing faces has an underlying link to an ancient legacy that I could only understand years later, when I copied the Fayoum portraits. Then I experienced the mood that suffuses the portraits, those vacant eyes staring out submissively at eternity. That same ritual is present, unseen, when a portrait is painted. It evokes the painter of yore who would enter homes surrounded by an aura of the sacred, for the roots of his profession stretch back to those who painted faces on sarcophagi in ancient Egypt. The ceremony as the artist is received in the home and prepares his tools is like a religious ritual. His ability to make immortality concrete is viewed with awe, and the person who sits for him turns himself over to his fate, trapped in a web of ambivalent feelings, with the reverential dread of the Day of Judgment, waiting for his own visage to look out at him from inside the painting. It's an uncertain moment. A part of him is severed under the painter's brushstrokes and steps into the portrait. What the artist embodies is not simply a picture—it's the luminous part of him that will be placed on the sarcophagus by which his soul will recognize him and bring him back from the shadows of death.

Painting portraits is linked somehow to regaining life, to resurrection. It's not much different from our modern-day illusion that we will cease while our visage remains. We'll live more in a picture than we lived in our bodies. The image is more eternal than the body.

I was obsessed with these thoughts and moods, though at that early stage I only knew them as a vague angst. Maybe those feelings were the beginning of my break with portraiture.

Amm Aziz, the Greek translator who lived in a house on the corner of al-Nahas Street, knew me from the days of the association collections. He had high regard for my mother and spoke with me sometimes. In the 1960s, his kids went to live in Greece. He refused to go with them, saying that he'd been born on this soil and would die here. His youngest daughter was compelled to stay with him. Amm Aziz had heard I was "clever with portraits." As I was passing in the street and he was standing on his balcony, he called me over and asked me to paint him.

"You have to paint me before I die," he said.

I went to his house on Friday morning, and he opened up the old, spacious parlor for me. I set up my easel and he sat in front of me in his three-piece suit. The painting took a long time. I was nervous, and the man had an absentminded look like he wasn't there. I tried to finish the portrait despite fearing it wouldn't be good. When I finished, Amm Aziz stood in front of his portrait, smiling. He kissed me on the forehead and then died that same night.

That incident wore me down, and I stopped painting portraits.

I was tired of staring at faces. I evaded the demand created by my painting in the city. There's a hidden temptation in every moment to see yourself in a picture, and I was tired. I sometimes turned it into a joke, saying that whoever I painted would die like Amm Aziz. The demand died down in the face of my insistence. It wasn't a conscious decision. It was an interior one I couldn't resist. I would tell people that I couldn't paint anyone because I felt I was the cause of Amm Aziz's death. They laughed, but it was the truth.

The thrill of painting that bloomed in me didn't desert me. It moved, by inertia, of its own accord. I thought about painting things. Maybe that would be less oppressive than faces, but things are beings too. A dilemma. Though things seemed lighter, they still had weight. I painted chairs, doors, windows, balconies, candles, the primus stove, the small kerosene lantern.

The lantern itself is a story. I grew attached to it. I took it out of its box in the kitchen and put it on the windowsill, and then on a small table. I absorbed myself in painting it, avoiding the goings-on in the house. From the margins, I'd observe my father sitting in the alley, waiting for Futna's messenger; the ruckus that Nadia had started making, now that she was in the third year of middle school and enamored of new pop songs; the silence with which my mother managed her affairs, from leaving on her rounds in the city to her return in the evening and sitting on the couch in front of the television. All of this happened at a remove, on the sidelines of the lantern's ineffable presence. It contained some secret I couldn't unlock. It was constantly changing, every day bearing a new expression, with its manifold lines and multiple textures, the supple twisting of its lines, the strange way it stood, like it was on the cusp of transforming into a woman. This was the most important experience for me in that period.

One evening, my mother went out and took Nadia with her. I got the idea to turn off all the lights in the house and light the lantern. I filled it with kerosene, lit the wick, and placed it on a small table in the middle of the living room. Its spirit appeared. I rushed to paint it quickly in the dark, with rapid, tense strokes, before the moment passed. I couldn't see the lines well. It was in my imagination, as my fingers fulfilled an ancient promise of light. The lantern was giving me its spirit, revealing its secret to me. As I used to say then, it was deep.

After that, things began to point to their spectral presence. I started to absorb it all and take it in, and I'd go for hours without eating, lost in painting. It was a bit of a mad turn, and it concerned those around me. When you're utterly absorbed in something that those around you don't understand, it calls your sanity into question. Were it not for my mandatory attendance at college and the private school, they might have thought me a lunatic. I was utterly lost in painting things, like I was treating the sense of tragedy that painting faces had left in my soul.

At night, when I closed my eyes to sleep, the figures would rise from their slumber and run through my head. Everything would shift and acquire its own special characteristics. If I'd spent a full day painting a chair, for example, the things around it would show off for me, feeling jealous. The carpet would fly up and attach itself to the wall. The teapot would twist itself into a burly duck craning its neck. The three cups on the tray would perform a mulid dance.

When the special nature of things reveals itself to you, you get a little crazy, and when you're utterly alone, without a helper or companion, you end up in a maze. My sense of things was so finely honed I was able to see their phantom doubles. A life force seeped into everything and it came alive. Every time you paint something, it creates a special bond between you and it, and it reveals its secret: chicken pens, chicks, and ducks, the gate of the house and old chairs. I perceived light under the rough, peeling surfaces of the wooden windows.

Rida Boulos lifted this fog when one evening he parked his new car at the gate of the alley and the sound of the horn filled the street.

"Yusuf! Tadrus! I'm going to kill you!" he called out in his cheerful way.

He'd seen the paintings I'd done in the homes of relatives and had come to chide me for not painting him. That day we took the car for a spin in the city and sat at a café on the highway. Offering excuses, I said I couldn't paint his portrait. I was sad because he was the most worthy of it. Rida's a true friend, my big brother and guardian angel.

That day, embarrassed by my inability to paint him, I told him everything and divulged all my secrets. I told him about my fear, the childhood accident, the serpents that appear to me at night, the flame that flickers in the dark room, and my father and the veil of estrangement between us through which he couldn't really see me, nor I him. I told him about my mother, and while telling the story, I saw the weight she'd unwittingly put on my back.

In his singular way of getting directly at the core of the problem, Rida told me that day, "You'll never fulfill her dreams this way. And you won't live your own."

He liked the portraits he'd seen at his relatives and realized instinctively that there was something alive in them, or a beginning just taking shape.

"You've got to live for yourself," he said. "That's the way. Dedicate yourself to your work and keep painting portraits."

I didn't believe him at the time and remembered it years later.

We became friends again. I met his fiancée and chatted with her. She was his relative and I knew her vaguely. They joke in the family that she put dibs on him when she was in fourth grade. We sat in his old family home on al-Fatih Street, and I met his grandmother—the head of the family, Rida called her. I went with him to Alexandria, free this time of the sense of compulsion I'd felt the first time. I was free. The city no longer had a hold over me because I didn't want anything from it. I just wanted to befriend it for a few days.

I fell in love with Alexandria again. We walked around downtown, went to the movies, and wandered the streets. Rida explained the architecture of the old buildings and we went to some exhibits. Mahmoud Said's painting *The City* enchanted me. These were the paintings I wanted to paint. That was the stuff of my dreams. How could I acquire the skill and insight to paint something like that? It was a long road, and portraiture seemed like child's play next to the Mahmoud Said painting.

I returned to Tanta feeling I would paint like Mahmoud Said. I won't deny it—I felt I could paint better than him.

Upon further examination, I hadn't liked the rational style of the painting. It was like someone had given him a subject to paint. It was like *Guernica*—no matter how much people talk about its genius, I feel it's artificial. It's true these geniuses had special abilities that enabled them to produce a unique painting, but my enchantment with Mahmoud Said's painting centered on the mood. It was the first time I'd seen the imagination painted, not in the European way of illustrating myths, where legends or Bible stories are drawn with realistic accuracy, people are the same size, and figures are seen from the perspective we normally see things. The atmosphere in Mahmoud Said's painting was the thing—a difference in the way life is seen. Look at the donkey in the painting. He's the most beautiful donkey you could possibly see. He's squeaky clean and sparkly, embellished, like he's just stepped out of a child's fantasy or a dream. My constant recollection of Mahmoud Said's painting made me take notice of the images that sprang out of my imagination in sleep.

One day, I woke up certain that I could paint pictures with the spirit of *The City*. I'd graduated from college and was waiting for my appointment as an English teacher. It was during the mulid of al-Sayyid al-Badawi, when Tanta is packed. The small alleyways are filled with women, children, and families, and the town seems different. I painted the teeming alleys, coffee shops, peddlers, banners, and the donkey carts in the hazy way of dreams. I painted another piece showing the procession for al-Sayyid al-Badawi—the Sufi khalifa, the standard-bearers, the tradesmen guilds, and the people lining the road—and a third of the Ahmadi shrine that resembled a sleeping bride swathed in white and green silk and surrounded by a grating of lustrous brass.

I examined the paintings, astonished at the beings I'd known nothing of before painting them. They'd been formed surreptitiously without my knowledge. I placed the three paintings on the windowsill, and sat in front of them. I didn't want to leave them, and if I went out, I wanted to carry them with me. I was so pleased with them, like I'd achieved my goal. The joy of producing paintings is as powerful as that of producing a child. It's yours; your existence made palpable outside of yourself.

That was in the mid-1980s, and the Ankh Society had broken up. Hazim al-Shirbini went to Algeria, and Hussein Said had gone to work in Cairo. Only Bilal remained, and he too was impatiently preparing to travel to the Emirates for a job. I wanted someone to see my paintings, another eye that could examine and assess these creatures. I needed an expert eye to help me see what I'd painted.

A couple of days later, I went to see Bilal. I climbed up to his house. He had a room that opened on to the stairs, with a small desk, a cot, a library of his favorite books, and one painting left from his graduation project. He looked at the paintings silently and then looked at me, a faint smile playing on his lips. I started to get nervous and afraid, and then I started to feel like I was sitting for an exam. I looked at the paintings with him, and though I wanted them to be worthwhile, they'd lost all their luster. They now seemed superficial, and there were some errors of perspective in the way the figures were painted. The notion that this was a test compounded my anxiety. Bilal finally spoke, in that unhurried way of his, saying that the visuals had improved but balance was still lacking. Pointing to some areas of dark mass, he said they were too heavy in that spot. Then he started talking about the clutter of the paintings.

"You want to say everything in one go. That creates noise, not a voice."

My sense of the paintings' worth faded, and I let him go on about the importance of choosing motifs.

"A person shouldn't paint every single thing," he said. "One paints signs and gestures, not everything."

It was more than I could bear.

"Sorry if I've disappointed you, but it's the truth," I heard him say. In his view, a good painting was about something else entirely, the opposite of what I'd done. I didn't have the experience or breadth of knowledge then to question him. In my mind, the gist of what he was saying was: Yusuf Tadrus wasn't born to paint. I wouldn't be able to do so until I mastered those elements he spoke of, and after so much practice, I couldn't do more than this. It was over.

I left his house. The street was a bit dark, the lamppost on the corner illuminating a small patch. A boy played on a bicycle on the sidewalk. Stopping, I looked at the paintings. I took the canvas out of the frame and ripped it up. It sounded like a fart. I tossed what was left of the paintings next to the lamppost and left.

It was a winter day. I crossed al-Nahas Street looking at the world as if it was again flesh and blood. Once fragile, papery, and dreamlike, its solidity returned. Things and people and relationships had acquired density again. A grand illusion dissipated.

As I woke up, the muddy earth from which I'd come beckoned me. I walked lightly on al-Nahas Street, not knowing if it was sadness or joy in my heart. But I was without a doubt light. As I approached the Mari Girgis Church, a feeling of freedom dawned on me. No longer did I need to sit for hours painting things or faces. I didn't have to devote myself to laborious, complicated exercises in the study of the projection of light. Life was unburdened now. I smelled falafel, entered a small restaurant, and ordered a sandwich. The tastiest bite of my life.

"For the prophet's sake, honey, keep your love away from me. . . . " I listened to the song reverberating softly in the homely shop with pure pleasure.

# Yusuf Tadrus says:

I was appointed to the Kafr al-Zayyat Vocational School. Every day I'd take the train at seven a.m. and return at two p.m. Working at a vocational school and taking third-class trains makes you feel closer to the earth. It smashes the picture you've created of yourself and the world in your insularity. You're just a nobody like those other nobodies. There's nothing sacred or special about you—you're just one of thousands who live without voice or significance. Nobody expects anything from you, nobody depends on you. You've got to live like them. This insight sank in and punctured the bubble I'd lived in for nearly ten years.

When you enter a classroom with rundown benches and see the broken windowpanes bearing the traces of the brick thrown through them, the walls made absent by a blanket of graffiti—mementos, declarations of love and loyalty—the boys with their yearnings just below the skin, yearnings to love and to fight, your responsibility to teach them seems absurd. The world I landed in was an absurd one.

I was comfortable being a cog in this sprawling mess. The boys just wanted to get their degree so they could go to an Arab country. The idea of going somewhere else obsessed everyone in the 1980s.

The work wasn't hard, but being in the classroom was a daily battle against the students' overpowering desire to break the rules and prove themselves against the authority of the school, which I represented. I didn't care. I was just a bureaucrat, passing class time doing anything, even joking around. If one of the applied ed teachers asked to take the students to the workshops, I'd immediately agree and take a break from the hassle.

I brushed up against the chaos and immersed myself in it. I was happy the notion of painting had disappeared. Sometimes, as I returned on the train, a farmer's face or a conductor's features would catch my eye and I'd want badly to paint them, but I'd shake off the thought right away. At that time, I took up with a group of friends who would meet at the Ottoman Café. It was a different kind of gathering, free of the austerity of the Ankh Society—just a bunch of guys with the same ambitions getting together. I knew Sami Abu Zeid, a theater director at the Palace of Culture, and so I regularly joined them every evening.

The world of the Ottoman Café was broader. There were none of the rigorous standards like the ones Bilal had applied to my paintings. Most of the group was interested in theater and music. Some were getting ready to work in acting in the capital, and others wanted to be directors on par with Youssef Chahine. Some of the guys were stragglers from the leftist movements, who'd gone to prison in 1977.

Life went on open-ended, empty, day after day, as if it would last like that forever. Getting some distance from painting had made me lighthearted, but I did seem strange to them, a good-for-nothing fellow, without ambition. Sami Abu Zeid asked me to work with him on the stage design for the play *Marat/Sade*, but I declined. I didn't want to come near the angst of art again. I wanted to stay on the shore and hear the distant echo. But the emptiness left by painting lurked inside me, coming and going in strange ways. For example, I wrote some short stories in that period. I showed them to the group and they liked them. I'd laugh at their enthusiasm for my stories. Unbelievable. Nothing was off limits—I told you, chaos. Until my mother died in an eerie way in the street, alone.

She'd been at the Holy Bible Association. She finished her work and left to do some errands before returning home. Walking on Suleiman Street, before she reached Ali Mubarak Street, she was hit by a donkey cart on its way to the wholesale market in the western part of the city. Can you believe it? A donkey cart! The cart pushed her over and she fell on her head, hitting it on the curb and causing a brain hemorrhage.

No one knew her. There was no one at the association that evening. An old woman who lived in the area said her name was Umm Yusuf. Where was Yusuf? No one knew. They took her to the al-Minshawi Hospital, and by the time she arrived she was dead.

I was at the Ottoman Café that evening, talking with Sami Abu Zeid about the set for the play, when a man came in asking for Yusuf Tadrus. I don't remember him. Can you imagine? I can't recall any feature of his at all. But I hold in my memory the sentence he spoke—"Are you Yusuf? Your mother's in al-Minshawi. She had an accident"—as if it had alighted in my consciousness without anyone uttering it.

I left the café in a rush with a group of the guys. Shockingly, she died before I got there.

The idea of it left me unable to breathe. I searched for one of her friends. I called Rida Boulos—he was in Alexandria—and Dr. Hani, and all the relatives, wanting them to do something. I was in a trance, refusing to believe it. Maybe there was some mistake. It was impossible. I'd left her at home before I went to the café. It had to be an absurd joke. She had to be alive. At the hospital they said they'd taken her to the morgue and wouldn't release her until the morning. I sat on a stone bench next to the morgue door, insisting I wouldn't let her sleep alone that night in there, but relatives forced me to go home.

My father didn't know. I saw him, strutting like a peacock as he entered the house calling cheerily out for Nadia. I probably hurt him that night. God forgive me, maybe I meant to, when I saw him entering in his freshly bleached gallabiya.

"My mother's dead," I told him.

He drew back as if ducking a blow to the head.

"Your mother? Who? Futna?"

"My *mother*," I said.

"The Sitt Umm Yusuf?"

He looked at me, but could no longer see me. I realized it from the way he was staring at my face. I knew the faint rays illuminating his sight had been extinguished and darkness had settled. The truth is, I was the sole cause of his blindness, once on the day of my childhood accident and again the day I informed him of my mother's death.

How did I survive that period? I was reeling. I didn't believe what had happened, like it had nothing to do with me, like she was at the association and would return. Then, when I knew for sure she was no longer there, the fear set in. I was completely alone. I discovered she'd been everything, that my peace of mind had sprung from her. When I became certain that she was really gone—that she no longer existed anywhere on the face of the earth—the world clouded over and shriveled up.

Every time I remember this period, life seems wan, as if it were sick. I'd look reproachfully at Nadia, now getting a business degree, as if she were hiding my mother, or knew where she was and didn't want to tell me. I hadn't known that she'd filled the space around me so, that her existence was what had given my life its meaning. Sudden death is hard. I was obsessed by the thought that they'd taken her to the morgue before her soul departed, and if they had let me in I might have been able to rouse her.

I stopped going to work and they sent me a notice of impending dismissal. It was a rough time. It hurt. Father Bula suggested I take a trip to the Wadi al-Natrun monasteries. He virtually forced me to go. I was silent the whole time, feeling her ghost everywhere. Nothing could make up for her absence— that was the painful part. I couldn't sleep, I couldn't be awake.

There was nothing left but slack-jawed shock, ready to swallow me. The idea of transience was weirdly, perversely present in that period. Everything is temporary, ever changing, and life is chasing after things that could vanish in a flash. I was in a vortex.

I spent those days alone, unable to stand a word from anyone. No one could help me, not even the Lord. I grew away from faith a bit and resented it. I often told myself that if she were here, she'd bring me back to my senses.

That time—not Alexandria—was when I was really weaned, and if I couldn't bear it in Alexandria, life was forcing me to face it now. I had to live on my own. My little sister was my responsibility, my father defeated, now fully blind, and my older sister now had ample opportunity to take possession of everything. I honestly didn't care about anything—let Futna take what she wanted, pile up whatever she wanted. Nothing would bring my mother back. Nothing could help me live.

Those given to psychoanalysis could describe my state with their technical terms and explain the matter of delayed detachment, but their analyses aren't relevant to my life. You know what? I was never ashamed of my attachment to her, and I feared her absence, because she was more present than ever, as if leaving had given her presence its full meaning. I started mimicking her way of looking at things. I was impressed with the depth of her understanding when I remembered her saying one day, as we walked the streets for the collections, "Pain is the salt of life. How can we relish joy without knowing pain?" At the time her bits of wisdom had annoyed me and I made fun of them, but after she was gone, I came to know with certainty that she lived what she believed and her good nature had helped her make light of the most difficult things and patiently endure suffering. She looked at the bright side of everything.

All of that started to come alive, and I felt she'd returned to me in the form of a desire to imitate her wisdom and live by it.

With time, pain eases, but I'll tell you something strange. Did you know that after I recovered from the shock and took stock of the expanse of life, I started feeling a strong desire to marry? That's another issue for those psychoanalyst pals of yours. Suddenly marriage became very important, and I discovered Janette's presence in the house.

Janette was the cousin of Sabri Shahata, who owned the scrap shop. She was my sister Nadia's constant companion and was always hovering around me. I hadn't seen her before then. I started to notice her, feeling her affection for me and her searching looks, and I'd find her right next to me, jumping up when I asked for anything, even just a cup of tea. She wasn't one of the girls I'd painted, but she'd been Nadia's friend since childhood. She had graduated from a business school and worked in the housing department. Brown, with dimpled cheeks, her face had a lovely quality. She was cheerful and obliging and often told funny stories about her family.

This link between love and death, can you explain it? It's like a creature defending itself against the specter of evanescence. Do you think that's it? Why hadn't I seen Janette before? Why did I only see her after my mother died? And I realized all at once that my life wouldn't be set right, that her absence would continue to consume me until I got married.

# Yusuf Tadrus says:

BELIEVE IT OR NOT, IT was Nadia who tied the knot for us. Janette would stay at our place until late at night, and Nadia would ask me to take her home, to the al-Gabban Market. A daily errand wrapped up in Janette's humor and her urge to marry.

She's the one who started everything. She's the one who clasped my hand and leaned in to let her breast brush my arm. She's the one who forced me to have feelings for her. She said she knew everything about me and wanted nothing more than for me to notice her; that she would serve me her whole life.

"I'm poor," I said. "I only have my salary and I don't have any other occupation."

"I know. I'll run the house on a shoestring and we'll save money too."

I listened to her numbly, but my fear and reluctance persisted, until Nadia told me one day, "The girl's crazy about you. What are you, a stone?"

I was afraid to take the step, but like I said, Janette's feminine warmth stirred the blood and flesh, and my life took the road it would travel to the end.

The little events *are* life. Don't believe there are grand events—all of it is minor details. Even those major events, we make them so when we tell them. The stories are what determine the worth of events and set one above the other. Who's creating my tale now? Me. I'm the one who is arranging the events, putting a glittering one here, a dark one there, one significant, another trivial. But the events themselves? They're all equally important.

I had other, ostensibly better offers of marriage, in the days of teaching painting at the private school and even through Rida Boulos, who said his cousin Suheir liked me. He offered to play matchmaker to arrange the marriage without much fuss.

"I wasn't made for marriage, my friend," I told him that day, laughing.

That time came with the emptiness left by Umm Yusuf's absurd departure and then Janette's presence, with her boundless love, lithe body, brown skin, and—my Achilles' heel—dimpled cheeks. That was the earth I wanted to wallow in—the conventional family thing wasn't for me. The day of my wedding, Rida Boulos arranged a huge procession for me.

"You're a free man," he said, as he took me to my new apartment in Satouta. "You made your call, now deal with it."

I moved to Satouta in the late 1980s. That area alone is its own tale. Next to the Church of the Archangel on Hikma Street there was an expansive space. Thirty years earlier it had been a wasteland, the property of Rizq Qusa and Boss Mikhail. Boss Mikhail owned most of the land, and he's the one who built up the southern outskirts and the alleyways around the church. A man would come to him and pay fifty piasters per square meter for a parcel of land big enough for a little three-room house. He'd end up paying fifty pounds in all, and then Boss Mikhail would tell him he could build him the house at such-and-such a price. The man would pay, say, three pounds a month, and the boss would build him a one-story house.

All kinds of people lived there. Street peddlers, horse-cart drivers, vendors of lupines and chickpeas and everything else—they all owned homes there thanks to Boss Mikhail. That was before a meter of land went for thousands. Boss Mikhail's house is still there next to the church. Spacious, taking up an entire block, it has a lovely façade. The plaster-work is still there. He's the one who gave the church the plot of land where the cemetery was.

In that area behind the Church of the Archangel, I moved into the house you know. My sister Futna rented the apartment and paid the key money, what we then called "foot space." Don't laugh. I love these words. They have meaning, and I often think of similar phrases. Repeat it to yourself—"foot space"—and you'll learn something.

When he was taking me to the apartment, Rida told me, "You're free to do as you please. You could be living on al-Nahas Street now; instead you're living among street peddlers."

"I lived in the alley and here I live among my people," I said.

He laughed. Whenever he met me later, he'd joke: "What's the news of the people?"

"They say hi, brother," I'd answer.

The early period of the marriage was charmed. Janette gave me all the love she had. I slumbered in silk, as the saying goes. I felt I couldn't want anything more than that. I'd go to Kafr al-Zayyat, come back home, do the household chores, and then take Janette in my arms. That period showed me the endless breadth of carnal urges, the depth of our bodies' earthiness. Janette's desires matched my own and soon the signs of her first pregnancy began to show. For me it was amazing that I'd be a father. That I'd turn into Khawaga Tadrus. Truly strange. I'd look at Janette's swollen belly in wonder—another being on the way. Because I felt a particular kind of anxiety about the act of creation, I was taken by the whole experience. I didn't believe it until Michel arrived a year after my marriage. Then real life began—the clobbering, they call it. I noticed my savings were gone, after my sister Nadia got married.

After I got married, Nadia had started spending most of her time with us in the apartment, returning to our house in the alley late at night. At a wedding, a young man from Cairo visiting relatives saw her. He worked in the wholesale trade and owned his own house. He visited me and told me he knew everything about the family and wanted Nadia. She could bring just her suitcase to the marriage—the rest was on him. Honestly, he took some of the burden off me, but she's my sister and I had to provide a trousseau, in honor of the Sitt Umm Yusuf. Futna helped me out with it. Nadia was overjoyed to be engaged. She has something of my mother's kindness and her purity of spirit, but she's a woman who loves love, who wanted to build a home and have children.

After Nadia's wedding and Michel's birth, I discovered I owned nothing, and my salary no longer covered household expenses. Children have unanticipated needs. I thought in this period about asking my father to sell the house. That could solve the problem. My relationship with him remained fraught after my mother's death. He'd abandoned the alley to live at Futna's on al-Sagha Street. There was no one to take care of him, my big sister said, when Nadia was getting ready for her wedding.

The house in the alley stood empty. Futna had paid off the other residents on the sly to get them out, and like I said, she paid the key money for the apartment where I lived. I thought the money was a loan and that as soon as we sold the house, I'd pay her back and still have some savings left over to help out with life. But that's not how my big sister saw it. What she'd paid for my apartment was my share of my father's house, and what she'd contributed to Nadia's trousseau was hers. As she saw it, the matter was settled. I'd learned this after protracted jockeying with her. When things got tight for me, I went to see my father at Futna's to ask him about the situation.

"I sold it," he said simply.

"Sold the house? To who?"

"To your sister, Futna."

"Without talking to me? As if I'm not your son?"

"It's my house, brother, and I'm free to do what I please with it," he said angrily.

"So if Umm Yusuf were alive, you'd have sold it without her knowledge, right?"

"Stop giving me a hard time," he said, exasperated. "I told you, it's my house and I'm free to do with it as I please."

I went to Futna, and this time she told me straight up: "You got your share."

"My share?"

"The key money for the apartment, five thousand pounds. That's your share of your father's house."

"Five thousand's my share for a house with all its outlying rooms in the center of town?"

"Look, I bought it with my own hard-earned money."

So my claim in my father's house was lost. He sold my share to my older sister and she didn't pay him a thing. She bamboozled him with a cash sum, saying she'd pay off the rest in time, and then instead of the rest, she gave him snow-white gallabiyas and care. But Khawaga Tadrus was no fool. He knew all that and let it happen, thinking of neither my sister nor me. I was saddened that he denied me my mother's and my share in the apartment. That sense of loneliness returned, thick and exhausting, especially when you have a young child with needs. I felt everything vanish into air, like I was flailing at the wind. Don't believe those labels—"father," "sister," and all that.

"Everyone has his own cross to bear," Futna told me that day.

I had no choice but to find work doing anything. I had some colleagues at school who worked as house painters in the afternoon, and I worked with them for a while. I was totally cut off from the Ottoman Café and my old friends. I'd go to school in the morning and then paint houses in the afternoon. Janette was worn out and took unpaid leave from work to care for the child. Life became extremely limited. I didn't want to go to Alexandria to ask Rida Boulos for a job—he'd set up a large contracting firm and architectural office. I couldn't. I found it simpler to paint houses than work for Rida, because I knew he'd give me an easy job to provide me with a monthly income. That was too painful and I couldn't bear it. When he learned from some relatives that I was working as a house painter, he offered to let me take charge of his work in Tanta and oversee the properties he was building, but I refused. I'd lived as I pleased and paid the price, and I just wanted to meet household expenses.

I was returning from work at midnight in the winter. I was too lazy to change and was still in my work clothes. It was dark and I thought I'd walk in the air and unwind. I ran into Sami Abu Zeid coming back from the Ottoman Café. He was taken aback when he saw me.

"What's going on, Yusuf?"

I laughed and turned it into a joke. "It's a disguise," I said.

We crossed the train tunnel, talking about the café and friends.

"Why'd you stop coming to the café?" he asked.

"Work," I said. "You know, the boy has needs and my wife is pregnant again. It's a busy life."

That was in the mid-1990s, and despite the fatigue, I didn't feel that what I was doing was weird. I'd come to terms with my life and had forgotten everything.

"You've worn yourself out for nothing," Sami said. "If you went to the pyramids and sat there making charcoal sketches for tourists, you'd make more."

"So true, Sami," I joked. "After all, the pyramids are right there next to al-Sayyid al-Badawi shrine."

Sami's shock at my diminished circumstances was unsettling. It alerted me to how distant I'd grown from the things that were mine. Sami was a director with the regional theater. He worked in the university administration and directed plays for the university theater and the Mass Culture Theater.

Actually, it was thanks to him, and some other directors in the provinces, that the love of theater was preserved generation after generation. They kept the flame burning. At least talented young people could find a space to express themselves at the university.

That day Sami refused to let me go until I'd told him about my circumstances in detail. We stood talking in Satouta Square for a long time. His astonishment at the sight of me unnerved me. I'd come home several times in my paint-splattered clothes, taken a bath and eaten dinner, and then slept in Janette's arms at ease. Why was Sami so perturbed by my appearance? I couldn't explain it, other than that he thought it a shame for me to waste my energy painting walls when I could do something else more worthwhile with the same effort. Was that what it was? I don't know, but he didn't let me go until I'd promised to drop by the City Theater the next day.

"Come see the set," he said, before leaving.

The next day I was standing in the theater. Sami had arranged a job for me in theater set design. Another moment of awakening. It was a return to the world of the Ottoman and its rambling discussions, a return to talk instead of silence and the smell of paint in freshly built apartments.

There's something stubborn in my constitution that isn't easily pried open and explained. Maybe it's the obstinacy of Khawaga Tadrus. There persists some underlying anxiety I can't understand. I wasn't comfortable working on theater sets. I was more at ease painting apartments. Proximity to art held a vague kind of responsibility. A feeling of some import, a kind of specialness, creeps into a person, and then the anxiety and thinking sets in, but I couldn't let Sami down. I worked on several plays with him after that. I tried to treat it as a job, distancing myself from the emotional involvement and saying I was just executing, not entering into debates. I'd talk with him about the scenery, propose some drawings, and go to the woodshop to agree on the specs and carry it out.

I wasn't so downcast when I painted walls. What happened to me when I started working on theater sets? Did the work awaken a sense of self-deceit and self-pity? I really was quiet and morose somehow, feeling on the verge of tears. No matter how I try to explain it, I can only say that I felt sorry for myself. Everyone around me appreciated my work. They praised the way I executed the sets—my ability to understand the dramatic situation and use the set to bring emotional resonance to the scene. I liked that, but it just compounded my sadness. I was always so happy to return home and play with Michel, to take him for a piggyback ride to the Satouta market to buy vegetables. It was a period of inexplicable contradictions.

The problem with set work is that it's seasonal. After the theater competitions are over, there's little to do, and government money is always late. It helped at that time that a law office asked me to translate some contracts. My knowledge of English isn't profound, but it's reasonable and I did the job. Some researchers at the university—also by way of Sami—sent me theses for translation too. I'd translate chapters of books they wanted to use in their research.

Maybe my urge to cry in that period came from an inner feeling that my life had taken a wrong turn and I couldn't start over and avoid the mistakes. Maybe it was that strange notion that took hold of me that I might have changed my destiny if I'd made a different move in the chess game life was playing with me. I was so, so weary. I joined a Bible-study group in a confession not my own. Father Bula heard about it and chided me.

"I'm not switching rites, Father," I told him. "I'm learning."

"Yusuf," he said, "I know your mind is big and you're searching for knowledge."

"No, Father, I'm looking for peace of mind. Believe me, I'm looking for my lost soul."

I've got a curious way of digesting what I read. When I start a novel, I get to know the scene and mood and the beginning of the conflict in the early pages, then I shut myself up in the living room and stretch out on the couch. I close my eyes and imagine the scene in detail, trying to guess the trajectory of events, what the characters are like, and the outcome of the conflict. It's a nice exercise that helps me get into and engage with what I'm reading. I tried to do this with the Bible, but frankly, I couldn't. The Bible has a strange energy that frightened me—some of the verses even terrified me. My mind played with me and showed me burdensome things.

My son Fadi entered the world three years after Michel was born. Despite limited means, the river coursed on and life kept moving, at least on the surface. But take note, there's a chasm in the soul where unconscious currents stir. You don't like such images. You're not convinced by this binary, but these are the notions that help me understand myself. Without them, I'd be lost. I'm not convinced that there's a material origin for everything. I'm not a zealot; this is just how I understand myself.

There is an interior chasm, something unquenched. Life is lacking—there's something unfinished about it. On the surface, everything is fine, but underneath it the specter of emptiness looms. A person knows it in moments of total absorption, in moments of unadulterated pleasure in everyday life, like when Janette and I had finished a moment of intense lovemaking, or were coming back from a wedding at the church or from Christmas mass. That's when I felt the wilderness surrounding my soul, the wind whistling through it. I felt life was brittle and weightless, and then alienation set in and I wanted to cry. Can it be understood like that? It will remain a mystery—an abyss there that says a person's life is lacking, meaningless, and that he's utterly alone.

# Yusuf Tadrus says:

ONE OF MY RELATIVES WHO worked in the education department persuaded me that the time had come to ask for a transfer into the city, after I'd spent nearly ten years working out of town. The man was kind and concerned about my future, and said that teaching language at vocational schools caused it to slip away and I had to become a real teacher at a school in town. He had a point. If it weren't for the translations, I would have lost the language.

I was transferred to the girls' middle school next to the College of Humanities. There's something more animated at a girls' school, and general education is a bit more serious than vocational ed. The whole country needs to be torn down and built from scratch. Anyway, at that school I had a romance that nearly wrecked my life.

The English classroom was next to the art room, and thanks to my old love, I gravitated to the art room and developed a penchant for sitting with Sana, the art teacher. With time, I started commenting on the paintings—it wasn't intentional, believe me. Sana began to notice and look at me with wonder, and she asked me one day if I knew anything about painting.

"It's been a while," I said.

But she stared at my face as if remembering something.

"The first time I saw you, I felt like I knew you from somewhere," she said.

"Souls follow their own orders." I laughed and went to my classroom.

Eddies inside me began to thrum. The desire for a woman blossomed there in the depths of the abyss I told you about. Sana was one of the most unvarnished, honest women I've known. She had a searching look and cheerful disposition, despite her quick temper. She did nothing without conviction and was stubborn in a way I've never encountered. The daughter of a well-known lawyer in town, she was trying to teach painting properly, and sometimes she painted, but her abilities were ordinary. One day when she was arranging some of the girls' papers, I found myself grabbing a piece of paper and quickly sketching her features. Sensing me drawing her, her face lit up and she laughed. She approached me and took the piece of paper from my hand, then looked at it for a few moments, absorbed, like she was seeing something that had escaped her.

"Damn, look at you! You're really talented."

The bell rang.

"Yeah, so talented. I've got a class." Then I fled from her gaze to my classroom.

The games of love are more alluring than making love. A friend of mine says the good stuff happens before we reach the bed, and maybe he's right. Love is a force that can turn around your feeling about life. It makes you thrilled to wake up in the morning, meeting the day with anticipation. Time moves, and each day is different from the one before it. To be honest, I have a propensity for such games. I like them and I'm good at them. Just smelling the scent of a woman I know well from the portrait days excites me and I feel an extraordinary vigor coursing through my body.

Sana was fearless. She took to me with exuberance, as if she'd finally found what she was looking for. She didn't hide her interest—she was open about it.

"Yusuf's a great artist," she'd say.

This stunned me, and tore me up at the same time. I started hanging out in the art room all the time after my classes. We started talking about ourselves. She'd graduated with a degree in art education. She had wanted to attend the College of Fine Arts, but her matriculation scores were too poor, so she spent her time just "bumming around," she said. She fell in love with art when she started teaching it. In her third year of college, she took a trip to Luxor and Aswan with a group of friends. She'd never seen the pharaonic antiquities. She changed on that trip, and then spent a full year studying pharaonic art. She loved ancient art. She went to Luxor more than once and had lots of sketches she'd done of the temple walls. She told me it was her relationship with the ancient temples that changed her.

"So you believe in the pharaoh's curse?"

"For me it was a blessing." She laughed. "I dream often of the temples." She fell silent, and her eyes welled up. She was choked up for some reason I didn't know. "It's a private experience," she said seriously, "that I've never spoken about to anyone before. You're the first person I've talked to about the temples."

We agreed we'd go to Luxor and Aswan at the nearest opportunity. Maybe the temples would transform my soul as they had hers.

She was baffled when I told her I'd left the arts college of my own free will, after just one year.

"No way!" she shouted.

She couldn't understand the family reasons I gave her and didn't see how someone could fritter away their future so easily. She seemed more upset about my leaving the college than I was. She empathized with everything about me, and this fretting and sympathy with my stories bound me to her. And she believed, despite this, that I ran my life by my own peculiar standard, concluding from my having dropped out of the arts college that I was a person who refused to walk the beaten path. That wasn't true—I'd drifted along, buffeted

85

by happenstance like a billiard ball—but I let Sana form this fictional portrait of me and I took pleasure in it after the years of drought.

By that time, in the mid-1990s, most of the girls were veiled and the sorting had begun. I don't know if it had to do with the wave of terrorism that came to a head with the Luxor attack, but I do know that the general mood started tilting toward segregation. People apparently got fed up with the hard life and staked out a path contrary to the one the authorities deemed best. I started to see it even in the neighborhood around me. Christians were now looking for a building occupied by Christians, and some Muslims refused to live with non-Muslims. It's a dangerous trend, because if it spreads you'll find wholly Christian areas and others wholly Muslim. But divine providence continues to bless this land. Barely, but it's still there. You still find a Christian in a Muslim building and a Muslim in a Christian one. Whatever. These things wear down the soul.

I wanted to tell you that the segregation had happened. So if a girl didn't cover her hair, for example, it was a sign that she was Christian. I got sick of that look people would give me when I said my name: Yusuf Tadrus. They'd look at me like I was an alien, just landed from another world. They'd search my face and steal a glimpse of my wrist, to see the blue cross next to the vein. If they didn't find it, they'd go back to scrutinizing my speech and face, and I'd usually get embroiled in a pointless attempt to show that I was like them, from the same streets and alleys, that I spoke the same language and knew what they knew. Ugh, so tiresome.

Anyway, Sana didn't wear a headscarf. Her hair was long, tied back in a ponytail like a schoolgirl. She was easygoing, but her gaze was piercing. She could melt you if her eyes settled on you. I'd evade her gaze; I couldn't handle it. My body would boil up and my limbs would go stiff—a scandal, if you know what I mean.

So life granted me an unexpected experience. Good days were hiding behind the emptiness left by my mother's death and the aimlessness of my soul, cast adrift between the smell of paint in modern, spacious apartments and the theater sets and the overwhelming sense of nothingness. There was Sana, looking at me with her searching brown eyes, longing, wanting to taste the forbidden fruit. You won't believe the crush I had in that period, a genuine infatuation and a sense of fullness, as if I were walking on the ground, no longer suspended in the void.

But the problems quickly mounted before the story could play out. Maybe the trouble even helped the story play out and reach its climax.

Spending so much time in the art room made people talk, and I started feeling like I was being watched at school. Sana didn't care. She hadn't done anything wrong as far as she could see, and there was nothing to stop her sitting with a coworker who had the same interests as her. This stubbornness aroused the hostility of a bearded athletics teacher, who clearly thought I had no right to anything because I was Christian. The fact of being a Christian stalked me everywhere. I hadn't felt it in my childhood, even in the tricks the guys in the alley would play on my father.

The athletics teacher no longer disguised his hatred. His look was clear: you're one of those Nazarenes, it said. I started to get a glimpse of the atmosphere my mother had told me about in the late 1940s, when her brother came back from Shibin, fleeing the mark the Muslim Brothers had left on his apartment door.

Even so, I was immersed in my story with Sana, shrugging it all off, until a teacher who wore the face veil started tracking me. Every time she saw me enter the art room, she'd quickly follow and sit with us. I laughed about it with Sana, telling her they thought she was a Christian because she didn't wear a headscarf. She confirmed what I'd heard whispered in the family: that some fully veiled women were stalking unveiled girls. Sana told me about one of her relatives, who'd taken a taxi on Said Street. Soon after she'd hailed it, a woman in a face veil got in next to her, then got out a short time later, claiming she'd forgotten something important. Before she got out, Sana's relative had felt a pinprick in her thigh. She didn't know what it was until she felt a sharp pain. She asked the driver to take her home and there they discovered she'd been injected with something that had eaten at the flesh of her thigh and left a large, swollen mark. She was admitted to the hospital for several days for treatment. If I hadn't heard the story from Sana, I wouldn't have believed it.

That was the atmosphere around my love for Sana. Maybe it was that mood that made us feel we were having a one-of-a-kind experience we had to preserve. It pushed Sana's defiance to the extreme.

This state of siege couldn't put an end to Sana's attachment, as I told you. In fact, it fueled it. She was impetuous, and whenever she encountered an obstacle, she plowed through it. Beleaguered and under surveillance, we could no longer sit together at school, so she suggested we meet outside school. Sometimes I felt her impetuosity would drag me down a road I was no match for, but I yielded to the resurgence of my soul, and her impetuosity helped liberate me from some of my fears. Your brother Yusuf is timid, but courage is contagious, so let come what may.

You usually hear stories about a Christian girl who falls in love with a Muslim boy, but nothing about Muslim girls who fall in love with Christian guys, as if it's shameful. Women are shameful in our country. I tell you, Sana defied categorization. The most exciting thing for her, above all else, was the forbidden fruit. And she saw something in me I didn't see.

"I can't stop thinking about you, Yusuf," she told me one day. "It's bizarre. I dream of you every day. I tell myself, no, it's impossible, Yusuf's married with two kids and from another religion. If I'm able to stop thinking of you when I'm awake, you come to me in sleep. Can you believe it? Yesterday I had a strange dream. My father had died and you'd come to the funeral and the sheikh in the tent was reading the sura of Yusuf. I called out to you and you slipped out of a gap in the funeral tent. There, in the dark behind the tent, were huge fields. I embraced you like Potiphar's wife, just like the verses say. I was afraid to lose you once I'd found you."

Strange. Her attachment sometimes saddened and baffled her. She'd fall silent, a defiant look in her eyes.

Sana had a small white car at the time. In the afternoon, she'd wait for me on Muhibb Street behind the public park. I'd get in next to her and we'd leave the city, driving down the highway. We'd talk about everything. The siege imposed on us at the school occupied our thoughts. During the day, we'd exchange words in passing and trade glances behind their backs, like teenagers. Sometimes we'd make a quick date when handing off a class to each other. In the afternoon, we'd talk about what they were whispering about us at school. She was shocked by the siege and insulted they were watching her. One day she said she'd been like that her whole life—whenever someone forbade her to do something, she insisted on doing it, even if it led to disaster. In the grip of love, I didn't perceive the significance and import of that quality of hers. That sentence passed amid many others. I didn't stop to understand it and know what I was doing. I was reckless.

I think that feeling of being embattled was the fuel that fed our affair and pushed her feelings to the extreme. Sana is the only woman who's ever openly pursued me. I'd seen admiration in the eyes of girls at church and in my days working at the private school, but such a forthright come-on, only from Sana. She liked the way I look. Ironically, I've long found my face to be a mask, a blank slate that doesn't reveal who I really am. That's another story, and the time would come when I'd paint endless portraits to be rid of it.

Sometimes she'd look at me and fall silent, and then say out of the blue: "Your eyes are so lovely, Yusuf. The color is always changing." Or "You have such a nice smile, Yusuf." Sometimes she'd change directions: "Yusuf, you're cold, you know? Your silence is frightening. A person never knows what you're thinking."

She asked about the personal details of my life: how I treated the kids and acted at home, how I ate and worked and slept. Sometimes I felt she wanted to know how I slept with my wife. She'd ask about the kind of women I preferred, the kinds of love I knew. Everything was fascinating and beautiful with Sana. Everything was delightful, sensual, and invigorating. Imagine, she was the one who took the lead in the relationship, who led my feelings for her. She embedded herself in me because of this eagerness, which I hadn't experienced before. Even Janette's love didn't have such flavor.

Sometimes we'd drive through the side streets, or we'd go to Mansura or Kafr al-Zayyat, or spend a long time along the Nile in Banha. Those trysts were dangerous—only a few women drove in the mid-1990s.

"Don't worry about it," Sana would say. "The story's going to get out anyway. My father knows people everywhere." The danger of it excited her and only stoked her attachment.

A person is weak before love, before this eagerness. When you're the object of such enthusiasm, you inevitably feel you're experiencing your one true love. I'm talking to you now dispassionately about the most important moments in those years, after the excitement has dissipated and the luster of those moments dimmed. Now I can understand and judge. I can invent excuses for myself, but I can also clearly see what happened. That love nearly destroyed me. Ironically, it wasn't the most profound love on my part. I was smitten with Sana, with her exuberance and desire, and I imagined I loved her, but in fact I was distracting myself with her. I'd recall her words and the tone of her voice as she told me about her life, when she was a girl at the American school, and about her sojourns in Alexandria in the summer. I'd remember her talking with the same enthusiasm about her favorite aunt in Maadi in Cairo, the closest person to her in the world, how every time she had a fight with her father, she'd leave home and go stay with her aunt for a while, to clear her head. I'd think a lot about her desire for a different kind of life. I felt she wouldn't stay in Tanta. She'd leave—there was no doubt about it—but she was waiting for the idea to mature. She had an irascible, fiery way of talking and you'd feel she was capable of doing what she said. She was angry and impulsive, always on fire. Sometimes she was very gentle and would fall into a heavy silence, but when I clasped her hand and embraced her, her breathing would become rapid and heavy, proof that she loved me. But her reckless sensibility didn't suit me.

My sense that she was the one in charge of the relationship haunted my feelings for her. It made me uneasy and stirred a hidden anxiety. I realized in some way that her feelings for me weren't about me, they were about her rebellion. But this realization lurked far in the background. It was an invisible barrier I couldn't see when I was in it, rushing impulsively into the adventure.

One day she told me her father knew she was involved with a guy. We shouldn't meet so much, she said, to head off trouble and take some time to reckon with what was happening around us. We had short conversations at school. It seemed the time for games was over and the time for seriousness had come. Sana seemed weighed down. I didn't know what she was going through—she didn't tell me about it. She was short-tempered and a little hostile. In that period, I realized that my attachment to her had become genuine. I felt I was immersed in love and couldn't go back to that chilly life before Sana.

My life had settled down and things were moving along their designated path. Janette started establishing her kingdom on my bones. She used me like a hired hand and I had to provide for the house and meet the demands. If I hadn't been touched by magic, it wouldn't have bothered me. If I hadn't seen angels weaving sparrows in the carpet in the workshop, hadn't seen the hidden nature of humans behind the faces, hadn't observed the ghost of things behind their placid existence, the life I was living could have been complete. Everything I did would have had a different meaning. I would have seen I was building my life and making a family, and every piece of furniture we saved to buy would have been a pleasure with the taste of a kiss. Michel moving from kindergarten to first grade would have been a momentous event. All those things Janette focused on would have been life. But they weren't. Her sense of ownership and the desire to forge a life created a weight I only felt when I met Sana. And because I'm a narcissist, thanks to the upbringing of Sitt Umm Yusuf, the involvement in life and its affairs denied me the romance I longed for. When the lights flickered and then pulsed during my affair with Sana, I raced toward them. Who cares if Sana's love wasn't a light, but a tempest? I was on the verge of losing my balance and falling.

In that period, the house turned into hell. Maybe news of the goings-on at school reached Janette. I didn't know. She had relatives in the department and the school. She'd look at me silently, warily, and in those moments she became dangerous. Janette was an inscrutable, colossal force, the archetypal woman, when it came to defending her life. You can't imagine her ferocity. She could destroy you. A woman defending her being as a woman, her home, her children, and her religion—an entire life. You can't imagine the dangerous, heavy silence with which she would greet me. But I was obsessed with a love that unfurled within me, overstepping all bounds.

# Yusuf Tadrus says:

SANA WAS ABSENT FROM SCHOOL for several days. I started sensing danger, a vague anxiety coursing in the air. Every day on the way to school, I'd hope to find Sana there. She was the one who could silence this buzzing. One of her colleagues told me she'd gone to Cairo. I felt she was pushing me to think seriously about our relationship. I realized things had reached the precipice and I had to do something, to make a decision. I had to cast myself into the sea and let come what may. I hardly slept. Sometimes I'd get lost and not know what I was thinking about.

How did I end up so far over my head in that relationship? Sometimes I felt I'd accidentally become entangled in Sana's story. She'd sprawled out in my mind, expanding and illuminating and swallowing all the life around me. When Janette would ask me to get something for the house, sometimes I'd come back empty-handed. There was a fight almost every day, but I didn't care. I'd enter my room and feel my life stopped at Sana, her way of talking and laughing, her labored breath when we kissed. Was my entanglement just a latent force Sana had awakened with her impetuosity?

I learned that the Church of the Archangel was arranging a trip to the Mari Mina Monastery in Maryut, and I signed up. I'd take a break from this tension and vague fear. I'd reflect on the love from a distance and maybe rid myself of it there. Janette insisted on coming with me.

"I want to be by myself," I told her.

"Don't worry, I won't bother you. I'll leave the kids with Mama."

We took the bus in the morning. It was a November day, the air chilly and the road hazy. It was a family outing, with kids, little girls and boys, and old people. The scent of hair cream and cologne pervaded the bus. The family atmosphere unsettled me, like it was a school trip. I wanted to walk the road until I reached the place of the holy fathers and get lost in thought far from everything around me. I was, in fact, at a decisive moment. I wanted to know what I was experiencing, assess and understand it, but that wasn't possible. It was a boisterous atmosphere, like a holiday, and my anxiety and tension grew.

Janette sat next to me, her body touching mine. I felt nothing—my feelings for her had been erased. But just remembering Sana fired up my mind and body. Are there types of desires? Some that cast shadows and some that illuminate? Strangely, my desire for my wife had with time turned into the shadowy type, merely a release of fluids and a means of procreation. With Sana, though, my desire seemed filled with light. Don't be confused by these religious expressions. I was sick of myself, that's all.

I felt light shaped my feeling for Sana, but ironically I'd embarked on that trip to rid myself of the light, because it was forbidden and sinful.

The bus took a long time on the road. The tops of the palm trees appeared in the distance and extended over empty stretches of land separating the hamlets from one another. The distant houses promised the traveler a life free of woe. My depression deepened and I felt weak—I hadn't even slept one hour.

Janette's attention was focused on me. I felt it, believe me. I knew exactly what she was thinking. She came on the trip to watch me, she beset me from all sides. I felt beleaguered and angry. Janette hadn't bought me, and I'd started the life I was living because I wanted to. More than once she tried to talk to me, but I closed myself off and held my silence. I didn't hear her when she said it would be hot there. I didn't pay attention to the meaning of the sentence and said the weather was lovely, and then I was lost in my thoughts again.

The bus reached the outskirts of the monastery. The faint light of the November sun reflected off the exterior wall, making it look clearer than it had on the road. Often the color of the light would excite me and I'd long to paint, but that was finished.

When you enter a monastery to be in the presence of the holy fathers, they say you leave your worldly self outside. You shed your robe at the monastery door and don another. The place has an energy. The Lord is there in everything: from the color of the light, the song of the birds, and the feel of the wind to the visitors' whispers, the monks coming and going, and the hymns floating through the air.

We entered through the large gate and I smelled the faint scent of incense that I loved. I was stirred by the color of the yellow wall of the monastery, the sun's rays reflecting faintly and sadly off it, like my thoughts. I stood in a distant corner, looking at the monks' cells and courtyard and trying to distill the essence of it all, which I hoped would grant me serenity. The monks walked here and there, some of them sociable and chatty and others brooding and stony, looking at you like an alien and leaving. I appreciated that. I appreciated that they were avoiding us, the children of the world. They were on a jihad to purify their souls of the foulness of life, trying to keep the Lord's light aflame as their forefathers did two thousand years ago. They had a responsibility to make sure the Lord's light would not be extinguished on earth, leaving the folly of children and empty celebrations to us and going silently about their sublime mission.

Every time you visit the monastery, you hear tales of miracles, and the atmosphere there lets you believe them. It's an atmosphere suffused with the sacred. The scent of candles, incense, icons, holy oils—you can believe that extraordinary things occur in that atmosphere, as if the laws of the monastery are not those that govern our lives. There, the laws of nature can be broken. It's a sacred space that embodies a glimpse of the Lord who created all places and times.

I stood on the edge of a group of visitors listening to an elderly monk with a thin face and a shrill voice who was breathlessly relating the recent miracle at the monastery. Under the roof of that monastery, a group of ancient monks had assembled, some of whom had lived hundreds of years ago, some of them from Upper Egypt. It was a strange night with no moon, the sky lit with stars, but their voices were audible. The abbot had ordered them to extinguish the candles. The ancient monks spoke at length of theological matters and then began to light incense—ancient types that no longer existed. They began praying in a strange tongue, chanting hymns in it. After the meeting, an old monk explained to the rest of them what happened in detail, for he knew the ancient languages: Syriac, Hebrew, Aramaic, and ancient Egyptian.

The miracle felt alive when it reached us, and although you doubt it happened exactly the way the monk described it, it's difficult to doubt that he himself believed it. It's like all the stories and miracles of the saints.

On such trips, I always leave the group behind and set out alone to wander the monastery. I wait for a special grace and try to inhabit the divine air. On that trip, I was still thinking of my love for Sana. The strange thing is, I thought it worthy of the Lord's approval. I didn't find it contrary to the code of the church. I wasn't sinning, and in my heart I didn't feel it was prohibited—that was just a rational figment lurking behind the teachings I'd learned. But in my heart, I knew I had the right to love a girl who loved me. I had so elevated my love for Sana that it had become the very breath of life, without which I would suffocate, and when weighing misery against happiness, religion must bend toward happiness. As I wandered the monastery, stole a look at the monks' cells, and watched the monks move about, my love seemed to me to be spiritual, despite its carnal tendencies, because at its core it aspired to what was beyond the body. There's nothing stronger than love. The Lord forgives in love.

In front of the tomb of Pope Kyrillos, which looks sort of like a saint's shrine, I saw a woman from the countryside holding a piece of paper and pen and asking a short young man with a thick mustache to write her a letter to give to the pope. The man was confused by the request and seemed torn between the woman's wish and his inability to write her letter for her. In the end, his quick thinking saved him.

I heard him tell the woman that this was a secret between her and the patriarch. She had to tell him alone, so no one else could hear. The woman looked at him confused. He took it upon himself to guide her.

"Get up close and tell the father your message and he'll hear it," he said.

"But I want to write to him," she said gravely. "Words fly and they may get lost and not arrive. Writing is better; it won't get lost."

"Bring the paper up to your mouth and speak your message," he reassured her. "It will be impressed on the paper, like writing. It'll be even better than writing because you can't understand it."

Brightening, the woman smiled. She took up a corner close to the screen, brought the paper to her mouth, and began whispering, her eyes closed. Then she approached the shrine and stuck the paper inside the screen.

I knew at that moment what I'd come for, what I was looking for. I'd come to write a message to Pope Kyrillos, the worker of miracles. I pulled a piece of paper and pen from my pocket and wrote:

*I know you, exalted father, are the worker of miracles. Help me be rid of this tortured heart. Help me grow close to Sana and marry her. You are capable of this miracle. You, exalted father, are capable of it.*

And I slipped the paper under the screen.

While I was observing the village woman, Janette had been observing me. I now found her at my side. I'd left her with her relatives, and didn't know how she'd gotten here.

"What did you ask of the holy father?" she asked sweetly.

Angrily, afraid the message would be ruined because of this question, I said, "I asked him to help me get a transfer out of the school."

I was sad, afraid, and baffled by myself. How had I come to believe such a preposterous thing? How had I grown so irrationally attached to ask for help I knew was impossible? How could I think the holy father could help me with something that was in any case forbidden under the rite? A betrayal of the religion? How to explain this contradiction? It's beyond me, but I'm telling you what happened. The strange thing is I felt the holy father would consider it, not from a religious point of view, but from the perspective of the human heart. He'd see I didn't feel the union was prohibited, and he'd agree, because a person's heart is the standard. "Consult your heart"—isn't that what you guys say?

Upon my return from the monastery, I experienced the serenity the body contains after being in blessed places. With cautious hope, I looked forward to the coming days, imagining things would go back to what they were a few months earlier. But it was the anxiety that returned with a vengeance, every time I entered the school and felt Sana wasn't there: anxiety, confusion, and an inability to ask about her. It was disconcerting, that feeling that I couldn't go near our usual places. My fears returned, as did my sense of beleaguerment. I had no support. Until one day Sana's colleague approached me while I was standing in front of the classroom waiting for the class. She told me Sana was in Cairo at her aunt's and that she would be waiting for me tomorrow at ten a.m. at the train station.

That night I had a huge fight with Janette because of my neglect and disinterest in the house. She vented some of her poison.

"You're selfish," she said. "I've never seen a person this selfish."

She was right. Maybe I didn't see anything but myself, didn't think of anything else. Maybe I'd lost my equilibrium and become prisoner to my emotions, forgetting the house and forgetting the children were growing and had demands. Michel was in third grade now, and Janette helped him with his lessons and watched Fadi at the same time.

Maybe she was right, but I thought it was poison she'd let loose that night. Woman is a mighty being no one can match. I left the house and walked along the directorate street, then sat in a café in al-Sa'a Square. I returned late at night after they were asleep. I stayed awake until the morning. I couldn't think at home. My thoughts were all focused on Sana. I was trying to divine her circumstances and what was happening with her.

I reached Cairo Station the next day before ten o'clock. I sat on the platform, tense from the exhaustion and lack of sleep, but feeling the rush of anticipation and joy. I tried to picture Sana after her absence. Ten o'clock came and I walked toward the spacious hall leading outside. I saw Sana standing in front of a newsstand perusing glossy women's magazines. At first, it looked like she was sick. She was wearing roomy pants and a maroon jacket, her hair twisted up in a bun. I stood a short distance away, examining her without her noticing, and when she turned, she found me watching her. Her whole face lit up with a lovely smile, and her black eyes gleamed, moist with what I thought was the normal sheen they took on when she was excited.

Putting down the magazine, she stood directly in front of me, as if she were going to fasten herself to me, and looked amorously at my face. She spoke as she took me by the arm and left her hand there.

"You have to paint yourself so I can take your picture with me. I forgot your features—can you believe it? In ten days I forgot them. Only the impression was left."

"We all forget features. Our impression of the person is what gives them shape."

She stopped again and searched my face with a serious look, as if trying to memorize my features. She was clearly ill: her face was sallow, black ringed her eyes, and the tip of her nose was red.

"What's wrong?" I asked.

"I was sick."

I assumed she'd had a cold. As we left the station, I started telling her about the trip to the monastery. It was cold, and the violent wind sent paper and plastic bags swirling about the buses and microbuses in the vast square. I told her the secret. In detail I told her what had happened in front of the tomb of Pope Kyrillos. I was trying to understand that remarkable moment when I followed the village woman's example, and at the same time was trying to reassure her of my love. We laughed at my naïveté—how could the exalted patriarch contravene principles he'd dedicated his life to?—but the tale followed us the entire day, a witness to something bizarre embracing us, an irresolvable contradiction. We were in the crevices of that contradiction, trying to extract the nectar we knew was forbidden and fleeting.

We walked side streets she knew well, all the way downtown. The gusts of grit had died down, and the weather turned silvery and luminous. She walked briskly next to me, her demeanor serious, asking me about school and what was going on there. I told her about what had happened in her absence and described to her my hopes and talked about waiting for a miracle the past few days. I described my feelings at length. She was silent, without the cheer and lack of inhibition she'd had when we toured around in her car. As we crossed against the stoplights and swerved to avoid people on the teeming downtown streets, she seemed sedate—a different side of Sana than the one I'd come to know.

We sat in a shop on Talaat Harb Street that faced an intersection crowded with cars. She sat silently for a while, looking outside. I asked her to tell me what was going on with her.

"I don't want to talk about it," she said. "Now's not the time. Let's enjoy being together and the talk will come on its own."

"I'll be anxious. Just give me a general idea."

Her eyes gleamed, showing simultaneous resolve and sadness. She clasped the cup of tea and turned it toward her. She told me she was under pressure from her father. He was determined to marry her to a young judge, from a family of prominent judges. They'd had an argument and she'd left home to go stay with her aunt. Her father knew everything about her.

"Can you believe it?" she said. "He knows everything. He knows the details of our trips. Can you believe it?"

She grasped for words as bafflement settled over her features. She couldn't believe her father was spying on her. He had visited her the day before in her aunt's house. He was set in his opinion and told her before he left the house, "You no longer have a choice." She spoke the words with a sigh, and with stifled anger and astonishment, as if she didn't believe she could be so powerless.

As she told the story, she didn't look at me as she had in school or during our previous rendezvous. She'd lift the teacup and hold it there, gazing outside through the window. She suddenly fell silent in the middle of the tale. She paused like that, as if she'd forgotten I was there. As if the echo of the words still puzzled her. As if she didn't understand what that meant—"you no longer have a choice."

I didn't ask for more details. She'd said enough. Our story had shown its serious, perhaps frightening, side. A sharp gleam and sense of defiance loomed in her eyes in those fleeting moments she directed her gaze to me. It was like today was the moment she'd been waiting for. Actually, she had hung her hopes on our meeting that day. I was perhaps her last refuge.

She looked at me and smiled.

"It's so hot here," she said, rising to take off her jacket and place it on the back of the chair. I spotted a red blotch on her neck and asked her about it.

"You noticed?" she said.

She pushed up the sleeves of her sweater and I saw other, similar blotches along her arm.

"These spots are all over my body," she said simply. Then, serious: "A kind of allergic reaction sweeps over your body when they put you in the noose." She laughed.

The sardonic way she talked about her illness made me nervous, and I didn't know exactly what she wanted, especially since, as usual, she didn't say anything explicit, just acted like we were meeting to spend some time together.

We went out in the street. The sun was absent. We wandered around downtown and had a light lunch at a small shop. We stopped at shop windows, and in front of the cinema she said suddenly, "Let's go to the movies. What do you think?" She smiled. "Any film at all, okay?"

I sensed her weariness. She was happy as a child entering the cinema, and insisted on holding the tickets and giving them to the usher. She went up the stairs quickly before me, as if the sudden idea of seeing a movie had awakened her life force, which had been buried under all the problems. We took our seats, and she told me her aunt was encouraging her. If she hadn't found some support in her aunt, she didn't know what she'd do. As the theater went dark and the movie started, she took my arm and leaned her head on my shoulder. I heard her breathing and felt her next to me, like she was a piece of me.

Human beings are odd. I was sick to death of myself, but what could I do? I was made this way. The clay I'm molded from is steeped in confusion and anxiety. What should I do with myself? Anyway, now's not the time, and I'll tell you about that in another story. I'll tell you about the emptiness and the way emotions turn like the seasons. Don't think I'm one of those people who believe everything is meaningless, grasping at the wind. No, not that, but the turn can be dizzying.

That moment was torture. Even now, I can't handle it, and even though I quickly freed myself of Sana's love, that moment never dies. That's it. How can you understand this? Sana is clinging to my arm even now in the darkness of the cinema, holding on to me. I can't forget the scent of the darkness in the theater, where her secret desire to be with me crept in and inhabited my body. Is the magic of this moment the inability to stay in the presence of intolerable beauty? Is it that very unbearability that makes a moment of your life eternal?

After a while, I heard her breathing become regular. Her eyes were closed, the light of the screen reflecting off her face, making it beautiful, tranquil, and absorbed. I didn't follow the movie. I didn't understand even one scene—I guarded her as she slept. It was perhaps the only thing I gave Sana, that hour of sleep in the cinema.

When the lights came up, she looked around disoriented, taking a moment to figure out where she was.

"Oh wow, I fell asleep," she said, wiping her face in embarrassment.

The frown and somberness soon returned, as she gathered her jacket around her body like she'd gotten a sudden chill. I observed the shift in her when we started to leave the theater with the handful of other patrons. She looked like she'd woken from a dream and would now return to her suffering, the full details of which she hadn't yet told me.

The daylight was leaving and Sana was still surprised she'd slept in the cinema.

"I dreamed of you again," she said dolefully. Not looking at me, she continued: "It can't be. I'm a strange creature, dreaming of you when you're with me. Can you believe it? It's like something's happened to my head. I'm not me, Sana, I'm someone else."

She told me we were standing on the balcony of a palace, looking over the Nile and wearing pharaonic clothing. Everything was quiet from the direction of the palace. From there, we saw the temple court. Her father was making his argument angrily, wearing the brilliant garb of judges. His voice reached us. He was talking about free will, saying the gods would not allow humans to behave as they wished in earthly matters because if they did, life would be undone.

There were two hours left before I had to catch the train. We walked silently toward the station, and there, in the cafeteria, we sat and talked seriously. She's the one who spoke first and laid everything out in detail.

"I don't want to destroy your life. It was my choice, and I know I fell in love with you without thinking. You're married, of another religion, and I can't even change my religion to marry you—that's if we agreed, of course. There's nothing else but for you to change your religion, and that's entirely up to you. I can't speak to that, but there is something you don't see and don't know. My family. Even if you were to convert and agree to marry me, my family won't let me be. You don't know my father. My family could do anything, even murder."

She was silent and looked at me before continuing: "There's only one solution: for me to go abroad. If you want to live together, if you find that suits you, you can join me. Anyway, my aunt's helping me and I've already started getting my papers in order."

She gave me a serious look and said, "Think long and hard."

She'd described the problem clinically, like she'd exhausted herself thinking about it. She'd figured it out like a math equation. That objectivity left me speechless. In truth, I was playing around. I'd taken the matter lightly until that moment. She'd taken the initiative, and I could no longer think of anything. The only thought that occurred to me was that she was arranging everything. She was thinking of love and travel and living, and I was living far away in my daydreams, slipping messages to the exalted patriarch through the screen of his tomb.

In the end, she told me she understood the sacrifice I'd make if I decided to go to her, but it was all up to me. She repeated that she wouldn't dare ask a thing from me and didn't want to ruin my life; the decision was mine in full. She was serious, going through the most important moment of her life, and her unbendable spirit showed itself. A maturity I hadn't imagined in our childish adventures on the country roads became apparent. She now seemed a complete woman, capable of saving herself.

She had declared her love, but couldn't force me to go with her. It was all too much for me, really too big for me, at least at that moment.

"There's a quarter of an hour left until the train," she said, looking at her watch. "I don't like goodbyes. I'm going." She grabbed a piece of paper and wrote a telephone number on it. "This is my aunt's phone number. Call me any time." Smiling, she put on her jacket. "If I do end up leaving, don't you dare forget me." She left quickly, with firm steps, and didn't look back.

That was a turning point in my life. Every scene is etched in my mind. Every scent, every color, the weather and clamor of the street, the tone of the voices—everything. My whole life, I'll keep loving Sana and preserve the details of that odd day. It's like a light in my soul. I've gone over the whole story hundreds of times over the years and see that I was impulsive and taken with her. I was anxious the whole time, and I didn't love her enough. I justified my fecklessness to myself, saying that she loved her own rebellion more than me, and that the whole thing wasn't really about me. Maybe that's why I could sever my attachment to her, because of my belief that I was just a catalyst in her life. She'd continue her journey, with or without me.

# Yusuf Tadrus says:

THE DAY AFTER I RETURNED from Cairo, I was summoned for questioning at the school regarding a complaint to the supervisor that I was late for my classes. A few days later, they questioned me about another complaint, saying I hadn't explained the lessons thoroughly. This was all ordinary, and I took it in good faith. I even joked with the vice-principal who did the questioning. But things changed when the school principal summoned me, closed the door, and told me they'd found love letters the girls had written me. She showed me a sample—I only read, "My darling Yusuf . . . ." I told the principal I wasn't at fault. For me, middle-school girls are children. I'd noticed some of them had a crush on me and others were quarrelsome, but I would laugh and deal with it in a friendly way, or seriously at times. Sometimes I threatened to call a parent. I saw them as youngsters. One of them might develop a crush on me, but for it to turn into questions from the principal raised alarm bells.

It all became clear a few days later, when I was summoned to the administration's legal affairs department following a complaint from some students that in English class I had spoken about Christ and read verses from the Bible. I realized something was being orchestrated against me, purposefully and systematically. I suspected the athletics teacher, but it was bigger than that, involving employees in the administration and education department. It had to come from higher up.

I took the matter seriously and told the investigator that I refused to teach the Christianity course and left that to a colleague because I wasn't versed in matters of religion, and that if I'd wanted to be a missionary, I'd have gone to Africa.

My life soured. I sensed a lurking danger in the faces of those greeting me in the morning and a watchful silence around me.

A senior investigator from the education department by the name of Naim Subhi visited me at school. He was a solemn man, a relative of Rida Boulos, highly respected in the family and on the job. The principal left us alone in a room. Mr. Naim closed the door slowly and sat facing me, sizing me up before apprising me of the facts.

"You know me, I know you. I couldn't possibly be biased against you," he began.

That preface alarmed me even more and I waited. The cold gaze he fixed on my face suggested he'd come at the behest of his superiors, although he was trying to convey it as a message from someone who was concerned for me. I grasped the matter in a flash and knew I'd fallen into the trap. It wasn't only about Sana. His story made sense of the air of vigilance around me at school. I started to understand previously incomprehensible things, like why my colleagues had avoided me, feigning business.

My whole life I've known that the signs of impending calamity first appear in the expression on women's faces; they have a nose for the off-kilter and can't hide their inquisitiveness. When I heard the investigator's story, I understood why they had been giving me peculiar looks. He told me that my story, in various versions, was all over town. The short version was that a Christian teacher had seduced and deceived a Muslim girl. In other versions, he had raped her and she'd been forced to marry him. He related the outlandish details that fleshed out my story at school before it spread to people's homes and then reached the bosses, sending a shock through the conservative city. In the story I'd become a gruesome figure, a Christian youth who ensnared young girls: someone they had to cast out as a danger to the conservative, tranquil city.

Mr. Naim fell silent and looked at me. He noticed my anxiety and fear, which I had no desire to hide. As if doing me a favor, he said he had found a solution. He explicitly asked me to request a transfer, not only out of the school, but the entire province—just for a short while, until things calmed down—promising on his honor to then place me at any school I liked. With a friendly, baffled manner, he spoke as if he were concerned for me. He informed me of the urgency of the situation, saying I might find myself in more trouble than I could handle. My tale was known at the highest levels in the department and had reached the State Security officer in charge of school affairs.

In a subdued voice, he spoke in methodical sentences, explaining dimensions that had escaped me. Ultimately, he homed in on the potential threat from some overzealous youth with religious groups.

"You know how sensitive this is," he said. "It could be your end."

He seemed sincere, as if conveying to me his own fears. Apparently I'd become extremely vulnerable. I sat before him in shock when he told me about Janette, my wife, and how she'd gone to the priest and spoken with her family about the matter. In fact, he'd come to let me know I was beset from all sides. He succeeded far better than he could have imagined.

He left me sitting at the principal's desk and departed.

Imagine, your wretched brother Yusuf had become a debaucher of girls, a vanquisher of virgin hearts. The exaggeration frightened me—I couldn't reconcile it with my own story. I was genuinely fearful. I couldn't get out of the chair even after I heard the school bell and the clamor of the girls leaving. The vision Mr. Naim had left me to contemplate was terrifying. He knew our weaknesses, what we say in our conversations and evening family gatherings, and as we leave church. He knew our vague fears, and he knew how to pluck the taut fear of persecution in the souls of all of us. He was very clever, because I truly felt that as soon as I left the school, I'd run into a bearded youth who'd ambush and stab me, and I'd die senselessly on the street like my mother.

When was I able to rise from the chair and leave the school? How did I walk to find myself sitting at a café in al-Sa'a Square? I don't know. My eye was opened to the fear in the heavens, beaming down with the sun's rays. It came from the sound of the afternoon call to prayer, coming from that area I'd played in as a child, next to the chickpea stand near the Ahmadi Mosque.

Everything had become scary. I wanted to go far away and hide my identity, hide Yusuf Tadrus from anyone who knew him. I was plagued by doubts and suspicions. I even walked to the station to catch a train out of the city, but at the station I again grew fearful. Maybe someone had been following me from the moment I left the school. I left and walked toward the fields behind the cemetery and left the city behind. It was a wave of pure terror. At times I'd snap out of it and try to contain my apprehension. Maybe Mr. Naim was just scaring you; maybe that's it, I'd think. But the terror would return in a rush. Was I that out of it, when the tale spread throughout the city? The religious groups were probably meeting now, covertly planning how to do me in.

I passed by irrigation canals and hamlets. I walked until I felt my body giving out. I rested my back on a tree trunk and shut my eyes. Night fell, and faint, distant lights glimmered on the side road I found myself returning by. Speeding microbuses would slow down beside me, scaring me and pushing me to the edge of the road. Reaching the outskirts of the city, I told myself that night offered cover. I tried to return home by the most out-of-the-way roads. I entered from the Mahalla road and walked along al-Ganbiya Road, passing under the Bridge of the Dead and cutting through Kafrat al-Agizi, then crossing the railway bridge until I reached the street. The fear returned, more powerful. Maybe someone was lying in wait for me at a building entrance. I scanned the road, looking left and right.

I entered my building cautiously. It was nearly midnight by then. I walked up the stairs and knocked on the apartment door. No answer. I thought maybe Janette was sleeping. Searching for the key in my pocket, I put it in the lock and went to open the door, but it didn't open. Janette had bolted it. I pressed the doorbell savagely. No one opened. I pressed it again and again, and then started banging on the door wildly with my fist.

"Open up, you bitch! Open the door! Open it!"

The sound of the boys crying inside brought me to my senses, but Janette still didn't move to open the door. I heard a whisper on the stairs. I heard Umm Said open her door and then close it. I no longer cared about anything. At that moment, I had lost it completely, lost all focus and comprehension. I sat on the stairs and cried like I've never cried in my life. I sobbed like a child. Said from the third floor, who worked at the mill, came down and tried to calm me down. I got hold of myself slightly and told him I was going to sleep at Futna's, but as soon as I reached the last step, I sat down, propped my back up against the wall, and rested. I could no longer move.

I stayed in that spot until morning.

It was frigid, and the images didn't leave me even as I dozed. I saw strange, disfigured faces and stunningly beautiful girls dancing, abandoned villages, fires blazing, the city streets damned and destroyed. I walked in ancient streets as the windows opened and people looked out at me in fear, quickly shrinking back when they saw me, as if I were the cause of the damnation. Children chased me and pelted me with bricks. I climbed a high hill and heard the sound of crows, looked at the sky for some promise, but it was dark, an endless darkness.

I don't know how I pulled myself together enough to go to the department in the morning. Entering with unkempt hair and soiled clothes, I went straight to Mr. Naim's office. Seeing me, his eyes widened in shock.

"What happened to you?" he asked.

"Nothing." I told him I wanted a transfer to the most distant place, the farthest place from here.

"How about al-Tur, in South Sinai?"

"Agreed," I said, and sat there gathering my strength to leave. Finally I said, "Janette didn't open the door. Tell her I want to get my suitcase."

I didn't forgive Janette for what she did to me that night. I was at the most critical point a person can reach. Someone who leaves one religion for another finds a welcome from one side and hostility from the other, but in my case, I found hostility on both sides. Janette launched a war against me from the side where I should have found refuge. I couldn't forgive her. No one can know what I experienced on that night of terror. It was a turning point. I felt I was nothing, a speck of dust.

# Yusuf Tadrus says:

MY BAG ON MY SHOULDER, I walked to the train station. I decided to take the slow train to Ismailiya, which passes by al-Santa and Zifta before arriving at Zagazig and then leaving the Delta going east to Ismailiya. I was weary to the bone. It's not just words, believe me, it's not. I hadn't slept for two days, and my nerves were frayed by imagined scenarios and fears. I was on the brink of collapse the day I left for al-Tur.

I sat next to the window. People got off and on. Students, farmers, peddlers in the village markets, men of all ages—misery. Cities came and villages passed by in the distance: a strangely vast world and a constricted soul beset from all sides. It's only by the Lord's grace that I didn't go mad in that tribulation. I was banished from the city and my home, afraid and cast out. I had let down Sana and was not worthy of her dream, and I had let down Janette and was no longer fit as a husband.

In my brief naps, brought on by the rhythmic swaying of the train, I saw my mother there on the other side and walked with her in light-filled streets. I opened my eyes angrily. The dream was rotten from the start. Everything that happened to me was because of the story of my birth that was implanted in my marrow. The falsity of being above life, living like your feet don't touch the ground, hoisted aloft in your own rainbow-colored balloon—all of that originated in the story of my birth.

I was learning now that I was nothing. You're a thing, small and confused, I told myself. You don't even know how to run your life as well as a puny ant. Insects and ants are better than you because they know, they set off toward their purpose in life without illusion. But this hocus-pocus left by Umm Yusuf's stories is the morsel that poisoned your life.

Sometimes words don't help you convey information. No, they usually don't convey, they merely gesture. The feeling of rejection, banishment, and smallness I'd experienced that day was bitter. The only word to express it is *bitter*. How so? I'd had a strange experience that day before getting on the station platform. It's difficult to describe. I'll try.

I'd walked through narrow alleys, divorced from everything. I saw, as I approached the station, that it was the end. Looking around, I found I couldn't understand what was going on around me. What was all this? Who was I? I looked at everything with bewilderment. This is a street—what does it mean, a street? These are people. What does that mean, people? Here's a chickpea seller. What's a chickpea? Meanings were severed from things, leaving everything unrecognizable. The stuff of creation prior to creation. Sounds, bodies, things, buildings, and so on.

Are these words the equivalent of what I experienced? Of course not, because I tremble even now whenever I remember that moment of hell. The familiarity we feel for things reassures us: we're where we belong. But realizing that you're out of place and that everything is as alien as the distant planets, that's unbearable. Listen, life is odd. I was trembling that day, on the verge of coming undone, but there's something in the human being that works with him. You know what shattered the alienation and restored the familiarity to things? A simple whispered thought: why didn't you take a Peugeot? It's faster and better. That joke of a question humming in my mind made things ordinary again. Odd, no? My mind operating at a remove, another voice responded to the question with a persuasive answer, as if they both existed somewhere remote from the vessel carrying them: taxis are sardine cans, space is limited. The train has more space to be alone in.

These voices conversing within me restored my equilibrium, though if you think about it closely, it seems enough to drive a person to madness. That day, though, the voices had the opposite effect, and I began following the train of thought they set in motion: So I'm still here, I thought. I desire and choose, even if I'm not fully conscious.

It was a hard day. I was utterly alone, more alone than I'd ever been—and I've always feared abandonment. Even the word *alone* sends an intolerable shiver through me.

Reaching Ismailiya, I took a Peugeot to al-Tur, my transfer papers in my pocket. I arrived at night. The city was silent. I'm not exaggerating when I say I felt relief just reaching that distant spot. It wasn't merely spatial distance, it was psychological as well. I intuited the city's features in the night, the ghost of the distant mountains and the broad streets with their low-slung houses, and my soul found stillness. The naps I'd snatched on the way helped me to hold myself together. I slept at the door of the education department until morning. A worker from Upper Egypt opened the door and led me to the general director's office. I handed over my transfer papers and met a secretary from Tanta, who invited me to stay at his apartment until I arranged for housing. By nightfall, I'd taken up residence in a three-room apartment in an isolated building far from the sea, with several other teachers. I was now far removed from my life. I fell asleep immediately, and didn't wake up until the morning.

At school, the classrooms were empty, with few students, and the silence was vast and deep, allowing the soul to examine its confusion and regain its balance. The balloon was deflated, emptied of all cargo save the pain of abandonment and disappointment. Even that pain, with the passage of days, became an idea and didn't sting the heart as it had in the early days. I was as silent as if I'd lost the power to speak, and I moved like a ghost among my colleagues. Time stretched out and the evening sea resembled a polished mirror, a still sea that drew its life force from the mountains and a profound sense of timelessness.

I spent my days distracted, given over to my thoughts. Things became clearer. My fears subsided and my body slowly returned to normal, but, like a specter, sadness still pervaded everything. Freeing oneself of rejection and disappointment isn't easy. You think you've done it, but it's there, behind events. It shows you its dour face in the midst of a laugh at a coworker's joke or in a confused dream of unknown origin. It lurks in the soul like a tumor you feel only when it's pressed.

From the first day, I put some distance between myself and my school colleagues and roommates. Or it was already there because of the pain I was going through. I spent most of my time sitting by the sea or walking until I was exhausted. Don't ask me what I thought about because I can't answer. I asked myself the same question. I only found scenes from life, now far away, and an ache throbbing in my heart when I remembered Sana and her face on that last day. Distance leaves an impression: it turns the pain into an image.

The school library had a small collection of books, which became my way of escaping the pain. I read most of them, moving methodically through books on religion and philosophy and ending with history. But walking remained more attractive than reading. Walking soothes the soul a bit. I'd return to the apartment after dinner, have a bite to eat, and sleep through to the morning. Even so, the anxiety didn't leave me.

In that remote spot, my Christianity stalked me as well, never for a moment letting me be. It was like the color of my skin, the features of my face, a clear mark on my forehead. There was no longer any need to mark me like my ancestors in ancient times. I was the sole Christian in the apartment, the school, and—it seemed to me—on earth. Our heritage helped me understand it, to accept it and bear it as my cross and salvation, but the weariness destroys the soul and I wasn't up to it.

I was adrift, nearly weightless, in the first months of my residence in al-Tur. Alienated and brittle, I'd see the gulf that separated me from everything around me when I happened to be in the apartment at sunset and my roommates would gather to pray in the living room. The gulf would appear, and I'd feel like an exile. The same thing happened when they prepared lunch to eat together. I knew what was said about Christians' food and its smell, so I isolated myself and ate alone. I didn't intrude on their lives, and I tried not to bother them. That's a tiresome life, too, like you're walking on egg-shells. You're always considering other people who see you only as a stranger. It was hard, but I didn't worry about it. They were young men from the countryside, about my age, kindhearted and religious. They'd left their villages for better salaries, or a quick promotion, or because the line to second-ment was shorter in the peripheral areas.

The days initially passed slowly and, for my roommates, with some apprehension. With time, familiarity set in, then peace. Gradually, they opened up to me and—confusingly— came to trust me. They'd consult me on matters, then tell me about their small problems and ask me to referee between them. This often happens to me, and eventually I become the keeper of secrets of those around me. I've never understood it. By all that's dear to you, tell me why this is. Why, in my relationship with anyone, do I end up being the repository of his or her secrets? Is it the silence and the acceptance? The refusal to judge? They're just words, but why do they trust me to this extent? It baffles me and I start to suspect there's some-thing going on. What is it about this face and soul that makes people think it's a safe place to leave their secrets? They even told me about their dreams. I don't know where they got such trust. For my part, I was sick and had bottomed out. I thought I'd divested myself of the trappings of the story of my birth.

A young, very ambitious man by the name of Nael al-Zughbi attached himself to me. An English teacher like me, he was newly married to his relative—his cousin, if I recall. He'd always say he just liked me, only God knew why. He told me everything, even secrets about relations with his wife and his trouble with his brother over the half acre their mother had left them before her death. He'd consult me in everything, admitting to all his friends that Yusuf Tadrus had an astonishingly agile mind. I laughed the whole thing off.

"Come see the mess I've made of my own affairs," I'd say. "Everyone's clever when advising others."

In that far-flung place, I came to know some details of small-town and village life. I learned about poverty, greed that justifies claiming another's rights, indifference to anyone else, and fraternal battles over a puny inheritance: a courtyard, half a wall, an inch of land. I heard comical love stories and saw people living life by default, vague fears driving them to accumulate wealth without any plan for spending it, just to build houses and buy land. I learned of resentments between brothers and struggles to go abroad. Oddly enough, God was always on the side of the person telling me the story, not on the side of the brother, who was typically the villain. I thought long about those stories, until I came to think that the life of a worm was richer than the life of a human being. People eat each other—that's what stuck with me.

I maintained my solitude despite these connections and long nights of talk, spending most of my time outside the apartment. I got together some fishing gear that I'd take to the sea every day. I'd put the rod in the water and sit there with no other purpose than to pass the time. The days were empty and crawled by. Events only gave me further distance and a feeling of abandonment. Everything had forsaken me. I no longer had feelings, as if I'd been left heartless. Pain and expectation had deserted me, and hope, too. I was as empty as the time I passed. There was nothing to do but wait for the first of the month to collect my salary, go to the post office to send the household share to Janette, and return to the apartment for another month of waiting for nothing to begin.

At the midyear break, my colleagues went home and I was alone in the apartment. I refused to go back, fearing another clash with Janette, though I longed to see the boys. I had the resurrection dream for the first time in that period. That day I woke up afraid, feeling life was precious and shouldn't be squandered, even if that meant spending empty days in front of the sea grasping a fishing rod that caught nothing.

The light was pure, like the very definition of light, as if the dark mountains had absorbed all the rays that make it heavy and dense, leaving only the weightless, transparent form: a liquid, divine essence. A brilliant strip of sunlight streamed in through the partly open window, spilling on the bedsheet and illuminating the room. I tried to dispel the strong premonition that I'd live the rest of my life in the monastery by looking for my slippers under the bed—any human detail to bring me down to earth. The heavenly world is forbidding, the mundane world companionship. The dream of resurrection was so strong that I truly felt I'd left my life behind. I needed to make an effort to drive away that conviction. I went into the bathroom and rubbed my body vigorously, as if rousing it from its slumber. I almost went so far as to masturbate, but was ashamed. I put on clean clothes and looked for a plate of beans in last night's dinner leftovers, then I grabbed my fishing rod and went to the sea.

I couldn't shake the dream. My childhood came back and I saw myself accompanying my mother on her errands. The desire to paint was like the desire for a woman, a carnal desire. Instead I tried to recall the journey from the beginning, from the paintings of George Bahgoury and the textile workshop, to Hazim al-Shirbini's atelier and Hussein Said's house, to the Ankh Society and the church courtyard. The details surfaced as if I were looking at someone else's life. The images flooded back clear and clean, like a sturdily built wall, each brick cemented on the one before it. Then the prophecy in the dream overtook me again. Me, enter a monastery? I shouted out. Impossible! I do love life, even if it's dirt. Trying to calm down, I told myself I was just exhausted by rejection and a feeling that I didn't deserve life, stemming from the guilt Sana left on my shoulders. Even considering a monastery was impossible. That's a life other people were created for, but I was created for the rough-hewn life I lived as a child in the alley.

Yes, let's say it was a glimpse of the light's magic. But a monastery? No.

As a reaction to the resurrection dream, the women I'd known paraded through my thoughts, the bounty of the vacation. It was an interesting journey, from when I first spied on Zinat as she was bathing to the woman who worked at the Palace of Culture that Amm Farid flirted with, telling him in a resounding voice, "I'll marry you, Amm Farid, don't worry. Let me enjoy my youth a bit, then I'll marry you." There were all the scenes from the private school and from when I painted the girls, Lamiya's face and her love. I was love-stricken, but it was a light, sweet love. Only Janette knew how to catch me— she sought to enter hell. Then in the end came Sana, leaving me with a stinging sense of failure.

As I sat in silence by the sea, I felt that my life was insubstantial, superficial, and weightless and that I was a slight being who might melt into the air. Maybe that was the wellspring of the resurrection dream. Maybe it was an inner voice telling me I had to make something of all this, to weave it into a carpet. But how, I didn't know. I didn't think of painting, because it seemed to be a time in my life that was over.

# Yusuf Tadrus says:

DURING THE SUMMER BREAK, I was forced to return to Tanta because my father was ill. I was dreading it, but a soft joy glowed when I remembered Michel and Fadi. The first night was stiflingly hot and humid, and I spent it on the balcony. My black heart hadn't forgiven Janette despite her solicitousness. I spent the time with the kids. Michel was in the first year of middle school, and Fadi was in fourth grade. I marveled that I had two extra bodies, two beings who could have a better life than mine.

The next evening I went to Futna's house on the other side of the railway tracks to visit my father. I didn't know it was his last moments. Like I said, my heart is black, and the resentment was still alive despite the years. He'd sold my sister and me out for Fatin, his eldest daughter.

He had lost his sight completely, but, according to Futna, would still tear into anyone like his youthful self. Truth be told, she hadn't neglected him. She continued to care for him until the final moment, always bathing and dressing him in clean clothes. She said that as of late, he was no longer capable of going to the chickpea stand and would spend the mornings in a chair next to the apartment door. He'd grown uptight and angry, saying with or without provocation, "I don't want anything from anyone." Then, patting his vest pocket: "The cost of my shroud is right here, in my pocket."

That evening his skin was wrinkled, his breathing labored, and his eyes closed. As soon as I entered the room, he knew me without my saying my name.

"Come sit here next to me."

I sat on the edge of the bed. He asked about me and work and why I'd left town. I told him, briefly, what he wanted to hear, saying salaries were double in the peripheral areas and that I'd come back the first chance I got. He was silent for a while before speaking.

"Umm Yusuf came to me in a dream, wanting to check up on you." Then he smiled and continued, "I've become the go-between for you two."

I went along with his joke, saying, "Tell her hi and that everything's in tip-top shape."

His features slackened—maybe he couldn't bear my cynical tone. It suddenly occurred to me that he was jealous of Umm Yusuf's love for me. He wanted her, and her fervent love for me, all to himself. That's what had thrown up the wall between us. The idea lasted no more than a few seconds because his breathing grew faint, and he lay still, his eyes closed. Then his breaths started coming in spurts and his lips fell open, and I felt he was slipping away. Afraid, I called out for Fatin. She rushed in and as soon as she saw him, she knew he was giving up the ghost. Flinging herself on the bed, she took his face in her hands.

"Papa? Papa? Talk to me, Papa!"

He breathed with difficulty and gave no sign that he knew we were there. He had gone. Only his slow, rough breathing remained. It continued a few moments, and then stopped.

I was standing near the door of the room, and Fatin was still holding his head in her hands and calling out to him. Then she leaned over his chest and started wailing, begging him not to leave her. I couldn't believe my eyes. Had I come all this way to witness the moment of my father's death? Unbelievable! His features were no longer alive. The man would never speak again.

Crucial moments electrify a person. Though they fade like any other moment, they instill a sense of wonder and a nagging knowledge of the fragility of life. It's my fate. What can I do? My wonder at it never ceases. I wished I could have had that moment next to my mother, not my father, but the strange thing is his death brought hers back to life, and throughout the whole funeral as I accepted condolences, I cried as if it were she who had died, remembering how she was left alone an entire night at the Minshawi Hospital morgue.

# Yusuf Tadrus says:

THEN WHO CAME KNOCKING AT my door one day? You won't believe it: Rida Boulos. Ah, it made me indescribably glad to see him. Rida's my brother and friend, dear to my heart. A car, some modern make like a jeep, was parked in front of the building. You won't believe, of course, that I don't know the makes of cars. Kids now are connoisseurs of these things, but your brother Yusuf is utterly ignorant on this point. I was as happy as a child. He'd grown fat, with a potbelly, and was wearing a gray T-shirt, but his face still bespoke his liveliness. I hadn't seen him for five years. Even when my father died, he was out of the country. I stood there looking him over for a few moments in disbelief at his presence in front of me, but he jumped right in, laughing at my disheveled appearance as I stood in front of the door in my pajamas, shocked.

"Blast it, Yusuf, you haven't changed a bit! What, time stands still for you?"

He was in a hurry as usual.

"C'mon, change your clothes," he said as he entered the apartment. "We need to be back in Sharm al-Sheikh before nightfall."

I changed my clothes in disbelief. He was the last person I'd expected to see.

We headed off to Sharm al-Sheikh. His company was building one of those small resort towns that had started proliferating along the southern Sinai coast. He didn't bring up my story at all as we drove, talking instead about the general state of the country, the opportunities for economic growth, and bureaucratic red tape and cronyism.

"How'd you know where I was?" I asked him.

He said he had asked at the school and they told him I was absent that day and described the apartment to him. He went on about his business in Alexandria, his work there, and his now-regular visits to Tanta. I asked about his family, and he said he had two girls and a two-year-old boy and was living a good life.

The first time I ever saw a cellphone was in the hand of Rida Boulos. We were nearing the end of the century. Life was changing and, in my solitude, I was living in a cave. The whole trip, Rida never stopped talking with employees and workers at the company. When we reached Sharm al-Sheikh, he turned off the phone and tossed it into the car. We sat at a restaurant with a roof made of palm trunks, the bay spread out placid and still before us. Such places weren't yet booming—they were still finding their feet then.

I told him I had a good life there and didn't want to go back to Tanta. I didn't want to. Every time I thought of cities, I found them claustrophobic. There was no sunlight there. They were dark, with narrow alleys and a dullness, and they lacked a vigor of spirit. I couldn't live there again.

"So move your kids and wife here, and live as you please," he said straightforwardly.

"And bring the grief on myself?"

"Oh," he said, laughing, "you just want to be an affiliate of the family, is that it?"

"Well, show me a way out of the marriage. It's a final sentence, as you know. I send them three-fourths of my salary. You know, I can live on virtually nothing. I don't smoke or drink, have no bad habits. Fit as a fiddle and straight as an arrow, religiously speaking."

He told me he lived a decent life in Alexandria. His oldest daughter was starting school, and he had a good wife who understood him implicitly. He couldn't find better. He laughed.

"Remember? She's the one who proposed. And she's not shy about it—she tells the story everywhere she goes."

But the most significant event in his recent life was the death of his elderly grandmother.

"I'd hoped to see you that day," he said, glaring at me. He was quiet awhile, and then said, "I didn't believe she could die. She was the one who kept the family on an even keel. When any of the brothers was in the grip of greed, they'd go to her to arbitrate. You knew her—we visited her once long ago, in college."

He said he wouldn't go anywhere without seeking her leave first. He'd hear her prayers for him and it would gladden his soul. He felt like her life was a source of bounty, and he thought she'd live until the end of life itself. Her death came as a surprise and confounded him, making him fear what was coming. Even a little avarice could put an end to his family's power in the market. Division is weakness.

A few days before her death, she gathered the three brothers and seated them around her. Each swore to her to yield to his brother in good faith, to not allow their disagreements to leave their circle, and to not involve their wives in their problems. They swore to never descend into internecine fighting and to preserve their bond unchanging to the end of their days to leave it to their children.

"Then the strangest thing happened," Rida said. "After my father and uncles had gone, she called for me and told me that I had to keep the balance in the family." He looked at me and said, "Can you believe it? She handed me the baton. I'm just one of the grandsons in the family. Do you know how many there are? Thirteen, and they all have businesses. We were all in the big house on al-Fatih Street. I sat in the chair facing her bed and she said, 'No, come here,' so I sat next to her on the edge of the bed. She looked at me with her bright eyes, her white kerchief drawn tightly over her head and covered in blankets, and said, 'Listen, I'm charging you with a trust. Don't interrupt me—listen and do as I say, even if you don't want to. You'll understand later and grow to like it.' She was silent a minute, then continued, 'You're the most even-keeled person in this family. Don't ever abandon your judgment. Reason and judgment are everything. I know I'm burdening you, but I know you're up to the responsibility.'"

Rida seemed to remember my presence and continued: "Can you believe it? She'd seen her death and was entrusting me with something I didn't know if I was up to or not. She told me it was my mission to make sure that greed didn't steal into their hearts. With a faint smile she told me, 'I'll tell you how. Be an example to them. You give in to them and then they'll realize how small they're being when they see you've yielded. Surrender is a virtue you'll teach them so they can preserve their bond. Don't be afraid of it—the more you yield, the more your fortune grows. The country's troubled and hard years will come. If you're divided, you'll be lost. What will protect you from the coming troubles is a strong bond.'

"I was awestruck in her presence. Her words spilled from her mouth like verses from the Bible. I knew she was wise. Her sudden illness didn't call for such ceremony—it was just a flu that had sent her to bed—but her tone as she spoke made me see death fluttering around her. When she died the next morning, I was afraid of what she'd said. Before, there had been the possibility of her recovering, but her death sealed her words and made them a fact, a promise that couldn't be broken. I thought I was incapable of following through, like it was a calling. It's tough, this business of a calling. It's a heavy load and it's better to be without it. But what could I do? She gave me a trust. The day she died, I was afraid of the load—I thought I couldn't bear it, and I wished you were there so I could talk to you; so we could figure out what to do about it. I wanted to talk to someone who understands me, and there was only Yusuf Tadrus, but he was far away. I was really angry with you because you weren't there in that moment, but I forgave you later. The fear hasn't left me since her death. She shouldered me with a load I'm constantly afraid I'm not up to, but I ask for the Lord's help and try. Every week I have to return to Tanta and visit all my uncles. I check out the problems and try to solve them, even if out of my own pocket. I visit Tanta now more than I did in my school days. Go figure. She bound me to the town and life there, and the promise is inescapable. Don't think I'm complaining. Actually, with time I found she helped me. My life could've been wrecked if I'd focused only on my business, on myself. I started to understand that by giving me the responsibility, she gave my life meaning. Yes, she gave me an additional load to carry, but she safeguarded me against the collapse and corruption that fortunes can breed."

He looked around. The sun had started to sink and the bay was a deep blue, glistening purely. He had been so wrapped up in the story he'd forgotten himself.

"Good grief, I'm starving," he said.

"I don't get hungry." I laughed.

He called over the waiter and asked him where the food was.

"Just waiting for your signal," the young man said timidly.

"Well, here's the signal."

While we ate, he tried to sum up the heavy sense of responsibility his grandmother's story had left him with. He was relaxed by my presence during the story, as if I'd taken on some of the responsibility with him. And it was true. As soon as he'd shared the story with me, his liveliness returned and he looked affably on everything around him. I'd always liked the capability he radiated, and he went on talking about life. Although his tone had grown more serious—a little more fearful and cautious—I felt he was more mature and open than in his youth.

"At first I was afraid to interfere in the family's problems," he said. "But I'm a pro now. As the days pass, I've understood what it really means to resist greed. I began to understand that a man is someone who knows that everything he created could be gone in a flash but he reconciles himself to rebuilding it and creating his fortune again."

I ridiculed the ease with which he talked about building fortunes when people struggled to find enough to feed themselves. He returned my ridicule.

"You're a twit, Yusuf. Why do you take fortune literally? Everyone has a fortune; there are fortunes in every life. A person may see his family as his fortune, or a friend, or anything that's valuable to him. I'm talking about loss and how a real human being is one who can get up again and rebuild what he's lost."

"Liar." I laughed. "By fortune you mean money. You were born into that environment."

"Listen," he said earnestly, "every kind of fortune, including intangible ones, requires seriousness. The best thing I inherited from my family's traditions is an allergy to profligacy and underhandedness. The family patriarch taught them that, and my grandmother took the standard and then entrusted it to me after her. Underhandedness can lead to ruin, so some of my family's personal ethics are part of maintaining the business. Carelessness, indecision, extravagance, chasing women or drugs—that could bring everything down. Work requires industriousness, seriousness, and discipline, which anyone who wants to build a fortune needs to have."

Then he laughed. "You know, I came across this notion for the first time in Kipling's poem 'If—.' You know it? An English teacher who doesn't know 'If—'! I read it one day in the Ahmadi School and it never left me. I could see myself losing a fortune and resolving to rebuild it."

He wouldn't let me return to al-Tur that night. We moved to his small chalet in the resort, an area of two-story structures and an expanse of palm trees and greenery. We spent the night on the balcony, talking about everything. We talked about the days at college, in Tanta—everything, and he asked me to tell him what had happened to me. He said he'd heard from Naim Subhi.

"He's the reason I'm here." I laughed.

I told him about my relationship with Sana. I felt she didn't deserve such gloom and gravity, and after a few months of living in al-Tur, I realized I hadn't loved her. I wondered for a long time why my emotions had been so strong in Tanta and then faded so quickly in al-Tur. I told him earnestly that I really didn't get it. I didn't understand why the love had taken such control of me.

I'm still incapable of understanding what happened, but I'm certain that the affair with Sana became bigger than it was and that my feelings for her were inflated somehow. I wonder sometimes whether the grim atmosphere of the 1990s had something to do with it. Could the general zeitgeist give an ordinary story a tragic dimension? I don't know, but while telling Rida the story, I was discovering that the emptiness of life and energy that had no outlet was the reason for my attachment to Sana. She was a wonderful person, searching for her own life in a country that doesn't allow individuality and persecutes those who do not conform. That day I realized that the best thing that had happened to me was my transfer to al-Tur. In the final analysis, Sana wasn't meant for me nor I for her. She was more attached to the symbols than to me personally. It was becoming clear.

"You know the most comical thing about the whole story?" I laughed. Then I told him about visiting the tomb of Pope Kyrillos and asking him to let me marry Sana. Ridiculing the idea of miracles, I told him, "The pope did nothing but grant what I'd said to Janette. I was transferred out of the school all right, but he ignored what I wrote in the message. He's only interested in preserving his flock, not in wounded hearts."

I noticed that Rida's face had shifted.

"Why are you sneering like that at the exalted father?" he said angrily. "He gave you the other solution as well. Didn't the girl ask you to go abroad with her and marry? See? You're unbelievable!"

That was the first time I saw Rida's temper, when he was defending the patriarch. He left me sitting on the balcony and went down into the garden to walk around the house alone. He returned awhile later.

"The patriarch showed me grace," he said calmly. "My son came down with a strange illness that stumped the doctors. I took him to the patriarch, telling him I trusted him and he'd help him get better. A week later, the boy recovered. Don't get mad at me, but it's by the grace of the pope. I don't like you to ridicule our faith. Honestly, it's the wall that shores up my life."

I was taken aback by the whole thing. How could that fortune, all those buildings and companies, rest on the tomb of Pope Kyrillos? It was a genuine, deeply held feeling, while I was utterly alone. I envied Rida his faith, his certainty in the exalted father. He propped up his life, and I was a doubter, lost and without support.

The next morning he told me, "I'll take you back before starting work." He was silent the whole trip.

"I was angry with you because I didn't see you there the day my grandmother died," he told me as I got out of the car. "But from here on out, please, Yusuf, if you need anything, consider me your brother. It's not just words, you know that."

I know that Rida doesn't get wrapped up in emotions. It seems he had a glimpse of the labyrinth I live in, just as I'd glimpsed the wall he rested his life on. He felt I was confused and adrift, like a shell washed up on the shore. Oddly, that was the only time we met that he didn't talk to me about painting.

Meeting Rida Boulos gave me a sense of companionship, and his presence close by in Sharm al-Sheikh banished my feeling of exile. I was no longer utterly alone—I had a brother there, on the other side. I spent the next few days in a good mood. We met several times. He'd call me at school and tell me when he was coming. We'd spend time outdoors, walking along the sea or sitting in an out-of-the-way place. We talked about nearly everything, and the time to discuss painting came. Rida thought I had nothing left but painting. Without it, the solitude would corrupt my soul and crush me.

"If you ignore painting," he said, "you're ignoring the most important thing in your life."

He believed in my talent more than I did, and he had greater insight.

I spent the next year in al-Tur, going to Tanta only a few times during holidays and at midyear. The last time, Janette called and said that Michel had run away from school and spent the night outside the house. I decided to request leave to go and see what was happening with the boy. The next day, she told me that he had returned and apologized and the problem was solved, but I wanted to see Michel and learn for myself what was going on with him.

I went to Tanta and we agreed to spend the whole day together. We walked around the town and ate falafel sandwiches, and I took him to the alley and told him about life here ten years earlier. We visited his Aunt Futna and went to the movies, and then sat at a café in al-Sa'a Square and played a game of chess. He told me what had happened. He said he hadn't meant to leave home, but he was fed up and bored for no reason. His mother had hit him because he'd torn up Fadi's math notebook and he felt like she hated him. In the morning, he went to school as usual, but hating the house, he didn't want to go back.

I realized what had happened to the boy. When Janette hit him, her hatred for me must have shown. She was probably taking her revenge on me through the boy without realizing it. I could have been wrong, but that's what I was thinking as Michel told me the story. He'd wandered in the streets until the evening. When night fell, he went to the station platform and sat there watching the people. Then he fell asleep in a train parked on the Shibin platform. He woke up at dawn when someone next to him shouted, and ran until he reached the house.

That day I talked to him honestly. I apologized for not being able to live at home. I said he had to take it for a while, and then he would grow up and could do whatever he desired. He said he wanted to leave, to travel far away from here and never return. I knew what the boy was facing at school, and I remembered sadly the difficulty experienced by a child in a classroom where everyone gave him strange looks because of his name. Despite my sadness, I laughed with him and made light of the situation. I told him he'd get used to it. He'd grow up and solve his problems.

"So just live with it," I said, "until you finish your schooling. Then you can go wherever you like."

I returned to al-Tur weary of spirit, not knowing where to put my feet. I was lost: no home, no nothing. How can a person live with this feeling? Believe me, I'm baffled. The feeling of being unmoored inhabited me like a shadow, but I'd still wake up and go to school, teach in the classroom, read books from the library, listen to my coworkers' tales and the sound of the sea at night, and grieve that I would never go back to painting. Rida Boulos was right. Painting had grown so distant it was like it had once passed through my life and that was it. Maybe now it could shore up my life.

I got used to the idea that I would live like that forever—that I wasn't an exile, but a prisoner, and would remain there. But I had the resurrection dream again. This time it had a different feeling. It was a Friday and the apartment was empty. The resurrection dream came and went as it pleased, with the same details I related to you, as if it were a prophecy.

# Yusuf Tadrus says:

AT THE END OF THE year, I was loaned out to proctor the exams in Ismailiya. There were women teachers with us—it was the first time I saw women proctoring the matriculation exams. They told me some women asked for the job, and it was their right as teachers. That first day, I saw the woman of my life. Love is a free-floating energy, untethered to any particular person; it doesn't rest until it finds an outlet. It alights on a target and goes to work, embellishing it and swathing it in a luminous aura.

When I saw Tahani for the first time, she looked like she'd stepped out of a 1960s film. She wore a blue-and-gray checked skirt falling slightly below the knee and a sleeveless, butter-colored blouse. There was no buzz around her like there was around the pretty girls. Her hair was parted precisely in the middle and fell on her shoulders. Her face was oval, with a broad forehead and a slightly pointy chin, and was without lipstick or other makeup. She looked out with a faint gleam in her eyes, and you could feel the fire of lust lurking behind her ordinary appearance.

You know, our mental image of sexy women comes from conventions, maybe from the movies, the exemplar being the sex symbol. We imagine that any woman who looks like her is *the* woman. It's a subject I'd like to talk at length about—the sex symbol and the ideal object of desire—but this isn't the time. Me, I know women from their eyes, from the way they look at things. I like women who are into sex. They have a kindness, a capacity for giving, and a generosity you don't find in a selfish woman who thinks she's pretty.

The first day of the exams, Tahani approached me.

"Are you Yusuf Tadrus?" she said mildly.

I smiled quizzically.

"I actually read your name on the list of proctors," she said, "and was happy to find another Christian on the team."

I smiled, and then she said, as if wanting to move past the initial awkwardness and signal an openness from the outset, "I felt some camaraderie."

"We're all brethren." I laughed.

"But you look different," she said, friendly, with the tone of someone who had long known me. "You're from al-Tur, right?"

"I'm exiled in al-Tur. What's so different about the way I look?"

"I don't exactly know," she said, laughing and scanning my features. "There's something different. I'll figure it out and let you know."

I told her I was from Tanta, married with two kids. I said I was there for personal reasons and I might spend the rest of my life in al-Tur, so she could consider me from there. She said she'd visited Tanta as a child and still remembered the scent of the falafel. Her aunt was married there. She had gone with her father and mother as a little girl to attend the wedding, in a church on a broad street near a granary.

For the entire duration of the exams, whenever Tahani walked through the school door, she would look for me, smiling when she saw me and gravitating toward me. We'd part ways when it was time to proctor and meet during the break. She'd sit next to me and pull out sandwiches, insisting I eat some. She was staying with her relatives there, but she made the food herself and insisted I break bread with her. Then she would stay with me until the end of the day. I was the only one assigned to that test center from al-Tur—luckily, because I wouldn't have been able to freely socialize with Tahani if my coworkers were there. She said she had refused to stay at the residence for women teachers because it was filthy and she preferred her relatives' place despite the restrictions. I told her I had to stay at the residence, as I had no relatives there. Al-Tur was far away, and so was Tanta.

"If it were up to me, I would have fixed you up a place and brought you to stay with me." She laughed. She said it in an offhand way, as if it were nothing out of the ordinary. I didn't wonder about the way she talked after she told me her story and started to make unequivocal overtures.

She was from Zagazig, married to a scrap dealer. She lived in the family house with her in-laws and the wives of her husband's brothers.

"You have no idea, the life of a sister-in-law," she said. "God spare you that horror."

The problem was that her husband could not have children and didn't believe he couldn't, so he blamed her. She had gone for a checkup without his knowledge and found that she was fine. He wouldn't admit he was the problem, and she couldn't confront him about it. She was afraid. He was liable to crack her in the head. Her father was a simple postal clerk, and he hadn't been able to refuse an offer for her hand from a man from a large family, when Tahani was in her final year at the Institute of Social Services. She barely managed to complete her studies, after begging her husband. The big battle came when she wanted to work. It created a huge fight, and she wanted to call the whole thing off. But after she realized she'd entered a prison with no hope of release, she told herself: Why not make trouble? Either she'd win the right to a job, or she'd return to her father's home. Her husband insisted she stay at home; she insisted she go to work. Relatives intervened and allowed her to work—being childless came down in her favor. She was hired as a counselor in a vocational school near her house. The best part of her day was the time she spent at school, where at least she could see and talk to people. Every year she proctored the exams through connections with a relative in the administration. She wanted to get away from the house for a while.

Tahani stuck to me like my wife. I liked the subtle allure that spilled from her, the tender way she spoke, her simplicity, and her delicate femininity. With time, her attraction to me aroused me. Your brother Yusuf is human after all, made of flesh and blood. He has needs, and I'd been cast out for so long. The few times that Janette, driven solely by the physical urge, allowed me to sleep with her, the sex was as bland as daily life. It was hard to see a woman receptive to me, asking me to embrace her, and not be turned on. I saw it every day, gleaming in Tahani's eyes.

The excitement I'd been denied for so long flooded over me. The body exulted, and I was again happy about life. Life was there, in that gravitational pull between a man and a woman. No words were necessary. Tahani walked with me, talked with me, and acted like my wife. I only had to touch her hand to feel the incandescence course through my body. She'd let her hand linger in mine when we greeted each other, and I felt the smoothness and warmth of her body through her palm, through the inadvertent touches that, little by little, became advertent.

"Do you know what's different about you?" she said one day.

"You figured it out?" I said, astonished, like a child.

Nodding, she said, "You seem like you're lost, present and not present, and you look at people from on high, like you see them from a distance. Right?"

"I'm impressed. How'd you know?"

I grasped her intuition at that moment, and I asked her to meet me in the evening.

"I'd give my eyes to do it," she said sincerely. "But my relatives don't allow me to go out except in the company of their daughter. They consider me a stranger and worry about me."

She pinched my arm in apology for my frustration.

The speed with which those days passed confounded me. I suddenly realized we only had two days left before the exams ended. I was stunned, as if it were natural for time to stand still instead of fly by. I woke up in the morning not believing I only had two more days with Tahani. I grew short-tempered, trying to prepare myself for a period of depression. I tried to put some distance between us, but she'd always find me, approaching me smiling and assured.

"Why are you running away?" she asked flirtatiously. "Did I do something to upset you?"

To be honest, I was embarrassed to tell her that I feared the end of the exam job. And then the last day came.

"What are you doing tomorrow?" she asked.

"I'll pack my bag and leave."

I guess the dejection was apparent on my face.

Looking at me, she smiled and said, "What's wrong?"

"I just didn't believe the exams would be over so quickly."

"That's what's bothering you?" she said kindly.

"These two weeks were like the blink of an eye, and now I go back to the bleak life."

"And if I told you I'd come with you, would you still be glum?" she asked coolly.

I looked at her in disbelief.

"Really, Tahani?" I gushed. *"Really?"*

"I arranged things. I told them at home the exams would end on Monday. I'll come with you wherever you go."

At that moment I nearly picked her up and spun her in the air. She saw it in my eyes and moved away laughing, going to sign in and find her room for the day. In front of the administration office, she called out, "Your panel's on the second floor. Mine's on the top."

I waited for her at the bus stop, not believing she would show. It must have been a dream, I thought. There's no way Tahani would come with me and sleep in my bed in al-Tur. I didn't think about what my roommates would say. That wasn't important at the moment. I'd solve that problem later. I'd tell them she was my wife and was staying with me for a few days until I found an apartment, and then I'd tell them that she didn't like it there and had returned to Tanta. Any old lie.

While I was preoccupied with figuring out her stay, I saw her standing before me. If you could have seen her face in that moment. Beautiful. A faint smile, her eyes wide and radiant, brown hair falling to her shoulders. Her supple body, perfectly proportioned, exuded vitality. I clasped her hands and held them between my palms.

We took a car in the evening and crossed over to the other side of the canal. On the dark roads, Tahani was next to me. I felt serenity and love. Forgetting the world, I didn't for a moment think of the trouble her presence could cause. She slept on my shoulder. It seemed she hadn't slept the whole night. I felt no embarrassment or any sense that she was a stranger. I truly felt she was my wife and acted with that certainty.

We reached al-Tur at dawn on Friday. Everyone was sleeping. We entered my room. Taking in her surroundings, she set her bag on the ground and looked at me, smiling. I heard her breathing for the first time. Her eyes seemed brighter and her face had become serious, absorbed. Nervous, I took her in my arms. Her body began trembling and she cried silently. I sat her down on the bed, kissed her palms, and wiped away her tears. Apologizing, she said she was scared and happy and couldn't stand her life. I embraced her and started helping her remove her clothes. I hadn't seen a body more beautiful than Tahani's. The proportions were a miracle. A lithe and pulsing body that felt strange to the touch.

The body has its own character, believe me. Tahani was a complete woman, but her circumstances had fated her to live forgotten with a husband she hated. She could only hope for death and try to snatch some measure of joy here and there.

We both knew this was just a brief moment pilfered from time, one we had built on lies and subterfuge, and we flung ourselves into love in this spirit. I kissed every part of her body, her breasts, neck, and belly, and her mouth and eyes, in gratitude for her. And she clung to me like it was her last chance to taste the joy of love, before the bleakness of her life enveloped her. As she came, she pulled me to her and panted. I experienced a pleasure I hadn't ever experienced before, believe me. I immersed my body in hers and she opened herself up and took in the pent-up torrent. It was uncanny how I was again a young man. I didn't go limp after the first orgasm. I held her again and kissed her, and I heard her say, "Wait until your body relaxes so you don't get tired," but I paid her no mind. I lost myself in lovemaking and heard her small gasps as she tried to stifle them in my chest. Nearly every drop of fluid imprisoned in my body was released.

You won't believe me if I tell you I experienced that night the communion with the light I'd thirsted for my whole life. The light that was a vague dream since childhood—it was realized in the form of bliss on that night. I can't explain it to you. Like the experience of mystics, it's ineffable, it can only be known by the person who experiences it. I knew genuine light, a connection with the hidden essence. Even painting had not had the energy that exploded within my being. It was magic.

Years later, when I borrowed Kazantzakis's memoirs, *Report to Greco*, from you, I read about the monk who passed through a village to gather seeds for the monastery, and how he slept in the house of one of the peasant women and made love to her until dawn, marveling at his bewitchment, and how he kept wondering if it was possible to perceive God's light through sin. That tale solved the riddle that had long plagued me. I found an answer to my question. I'd often wondered if one could connect with the soul through means other than conventional religious ones. Was it possible? Tahani gave me a glimpse of the light. She showed me how a woman could be, a spirit of abundant generosity underneath an austere life. I'm still grateful to her, even though things became muddied and I never experienced that ecstasy again.

She refused to return to Ismailiya on Sunday and stayed with me a full week. It was paradise I saw and lived. But my roommates complained. They somehow knew that Tahani wasn't my wife, and a teacher from Tanta who knew my family informed my roommates that she wasn't. I felt the tension in the apartment. I asked Tahani to pack her bag and took her to the station to return to Ismailiya so I could devote myself to dealing with the problems her presence there had created.

You know the sensitivity and male jealousy around such things. My roommates forgot all the friendship between us and put me on trial. In unison they yelled that they weren't cuckolds and that I'd taken them for fools. I had no response. I told them I'd wronged them and was prepared to accept any judgment to placate them. Can you believe not one of them took my side? I knew it would happen. Even Nabil, the one I'd imagined was closest to me, seemed fearful and couldn't resist the tide. He began glaring at me more angrily than anyone else, as if I'd gotten him into something over his head. As if I'd exposed his own weakness with my behavior. He was the most hostile of all.

"You think he's Moses but he turns out to be Pharaoh," he sneered.

Attempting to calm things down, I said again I was wrong and would accept any judgment. Then I went to my room and fell asleep immediately, contented, undisturbed by their hostility. I'd long grown familiar with them and knew how they thought. I left them to discuss what to do about me, and in the evening, the oldest one informed me that there was no longer a place for me in the apartment and that they were giving me three days to find somewhere else to stay.

I told a worker in the administration from Sohag, a friend, that I was no longer comfortable in the apartment and wanted somewhere else to stay.

"When you want to go catting around, tell me and I'll help," he said, smiling. "You're a rookie. Taking a woman into a bachelors' apartment?"

I discovered the entire administration knew. You're apparently destined for scandal everywhere, Yusuf. Actually, I was sick of eyes peering into my life and sick of feeling embattled.

"Do you have another apartment?" I snapped.

"Give me one day."

The next evening he told me, "You're in luck," and took me to a small apartment inhabited by an engineer with an oil company. His work took him to the desert for long periods and he only returned to al-Tur a few days a month. I moved my things into the new apartment and found relief far from all that stress. At school I paid no mind to my coworkers' looks. I was alone again and didn't want to know anyone.

My first night in the new apartment, I went to sleep depressed. Tahani's abrupt departure showed me I hadn't yet had enough of her. That night I dreamed she was still in my room. I tried to scoot over to make room for her next to me on the bed. There were ringing sounds in the air, sounds I hadn't initially noticed, the brassy sound of distant trumpets. I sat on the edge of the bed contemplating Tahani. She was sleeping on her stomach, a body of marble. I told myself painting was the greatest gift from the Lord, that it was the talent that could protect a person from temptation. I don't know how I imagined the scene to be real. Then I slept next to her in the dream and dreamed of her naked, sitting on a stone in the sea, swinging her legs. The balanced proportions of her body, the smoothness of its lines, and the softness of its touch were enough to make a person think she was the first woman. But then Janette appeared with her brother Nagib and several members of her family. They crossed the road and called out to me, dampening the splendor of the moment. I spun around to meet them so they wouldn't see Tahani, and in the same second I heard her scream. I saw a huge serpent come out from under the rock, heading her way. I flew to her and took her in my arms, then I lifted her off the stone and flew away with her, the serpent behind us. We were faster than it was, happy that we were outpacing it and certain that it wouldn't catch us. We landed in a foggy spot. The sound of the trumpets was farther away now, but still lingered in the air. I smelled the scent of earth and felt the rippling of the nearby river. The river's close, I said and, leaning back her head, she said, I know. There were palm trees spreading out to the horizon. Long grasses ending in tassels like cattails and a dense wood surrounded a straw hut. Tahani went in to get dressed. We heard the chirping of strange birds, but our fear of the serpent persisted like a shadow between us. It's the sin chasing us, Tahani said. I'm going back to my husband. Then I found myself at a provincial bus stop putting her in an old Ford, standing there like in a scene from a black-and-white movie.

A few days later, Mr. Naim, and with him Janette's brother Nagib, knocked on the apartment door in al-Tur. When I saw him standing there—with his towering frame and serious face, his thin mustache lining the edge of his lip, and his starched three-piece suit—I knew my fate. I knew I shouldn't resist and must accept what he offered. His smooth way of encapsulating things compelled you to choose as he did. I opened up the living room for them, and since they had just finished the journey, I proposed we have a bite to eat and talk at our leisure. The night was long, after all. I was trying to find an opportunity to focus, but like I said, as soon as Mr. Naim shows up, there's nothing you can do. The air was charged with irritation and tension. Nagib was belligerent as he talked about how I'd left the boys and come here to live as I pleased.

"Ask this kind man here," I said. "He's the one who proposed I transfer myself out of the governorate."

That night, Mr. Naim laid the matter out with his customary wisdom. Janette could no longer handle raising the boys alone. The responsibility was too much for her, and the cause of my transfer to al-Tur was no longer relevant. The art teacher had left the education department and traveled abroad long ago. There were no longer any fears, since after all these years people had forgotten the story. He steered the entire conversation to the kids, and how my presence at home had become necessary now. Though Mr. Naim tried to sugar-coat it, Janette loomed behind the demand: her bird—her property—could not be left at large. The cage had been read-ied; it was time to clip his wings and tame him.

I asked for time to think. The vacation was long, and the transfer could go through at the beginning of the term.

# Yusuf Tadrus says:

I WAS ALONE AGAIN. I passed empty days walking in the sun and resenting myself. I'd get up in the morning and leave the house, looking for a place to find some tranquility. I could only stay a short time in one place. I'd go to the school. On the break, only one worker and secretary were there. I'd walk toward the beach, but would soon return to the city and sit at a coffee shop, the flies buzzing around me. It was so hot, I'd return to the apartment exhausted, sleep a bit, and wake up, realizing that Tahani's departure had taken the shine off the city.

Gradually my condition worsened. After having been able to sit by the sea for hours, I couldn't stay there more than a few minutes. It was a dark, empty time, and the city closed in on me. How had I stood it all that time? The stagnant sea, the forbidding, distant mountain, and recruits temporarily passing through for boot camp. The sight of Tahani never left me. The novelty of it all and that it had ended so hastily stunned me. I couldn't believe the story ended there. Of course, other thoughts plagued me, too: What exactly do you want? The woman's living in her hometown. Yes, her life is suffocating, but she can't up and leave her life. And you've got kids. That clarity of mind would quickly fade, though, and the confusion return. For the first time, I even considered visiting the ancient church in al-Tur, which I hadn't once visited in my stay there. I quickly reconsidered. I wasn't naïve after all. My pain was no one else's concern. My misery was of my own making, the fault of my desire that flourished on the margins, there where the impossible lived. I had to face the consequences.

In the end, I couldn't stand not seeing Tahani. The very idea of it was taxing. I decided to go to Zagazig, however it turned out. Tahani had left me her sister's phone number, and I knew the name of her school. I could come up with any excuse, invent some lie to see her. I was afraid I'd lost the piece of paper. She wrote the number for me before getting in the car back to Ismailiya. Her hand had put the slip of paper in my shirt pocket as she said, "Maybe circumstances will permit. Who knows?"

I looked for the shirt and found it bundled with the laundry I put off doing every day. I sat looking at the numbers written in Tahani's scrawl, picturing her.

I calmed down some and thought about what was happening to me. I found my own behavior odd, impulsive, as if I'd woken from a dream and had to recapture it. How could I be so deranged? To think of going to Zagazig and meeting Tahani, come what may? But there was nothing to bring me relief, save seeing her and taking her away somewhere. See? The impossible is compelling. The impossible is there, where death is. But can you imagine, that madness is what gave my life meaning—my knowledge that it was impossible. Even so, something inside me propelled me toward it, endangering my life and hers. It was utter madness. She'd described her circumstances, how she was encircled by relatives and acquaintances. I risked facing trouble of the sort I hadn't been able to handle with Sana. Nevertheless, I hadn't learned, and I rushed blindly ahead.

The city seemed exciting again. I went to the telephone exchange that evening and dialed the number. I waited until the long-distance bell rang and entered the phone booth. My heart racing, I waited to hear the voice of Tahani's sister, so I could tell her what I'd thought out at length. I'd beseech her to tell Tahani that I was dying and that I wanted to see her just one more time, but I heard a rough male voice aggressively saying, "Hello? Hello!" The tone roused me from my daydreams and I quickly hung up. I saw in a flash the risks I was taking for myself and for Tahani.

I sat in the exchange, disappointed and fearful, as if that voice might come out at me from the telephone set, like it had known me. The fear annoyed me, and I told myself I'd call again, not believing that nascent hope could be dispelled so quickly. Consoling myself, I said I'd wait awhile—men usually leave the house in the evening. I could call again at seven p.m. I left the telephone exchange distressed. The journey back to the apartment seemed endless. My body was heavy and my spirit subdued. I opened the apartment and stretched out on the couch in the living room, unable to breathe. Impossible for hope to be extinguished so quickly.

In the evening, I went back to the exchange and called the number again. Fearfully, I waited for the long buzz of the ringer to stop. I picked up the receiver anyway and heard the low voice of a woman. I waited until I heard "hello" several times, then, fearing she would hang up, I spoke hastily.

"This is Yusuf Tadrus, a colleague of Tahani."

I paused, the silence heavy, but words poured out of me.

"Please, I want to talk to Tahani. Please."

I spoke imploringly, miserably beseeching her, as if some force field in the heavens had opened and I feared it would close. I don't know what happened to me. Didn't I tell you I was beside myself? I saw myself acting, detached from myself, and I was enthralled, doing the self's bidding like a zombie, unable to resist.

"Tahani is very sick," I heard the woman's voice say. "She won't be going to school these days."

"Can't I talk to her?"

"No, you can't," she said resolutely. "I told you, she's very sick."

I was silent, not knowing what to do.

"Listen," she said, "Tahani's life is hard and you're putting her in danger by calling. Please, if you really care for her, stop calling."

I found no words to respond.

I heard her say, insisting on making things clear, "Her husband could kill her."

"Fine, I won't call her, but how can I see her? I'll just see her from a distance."

Her sister sighed. "Tahani goes to school on Tuesday and Thursday." Then she swiftly hung up.

I again sat there in the hall of the telephone exchange, even more tired than I was that morning.

The city was so claustrophobic I could no longer breathe. Three days passed as I lay there, unable to sleep. The idea that I wouldn't be able to see Tahani ached like a physical pain. I went to a nearby pharmacy and asked for a sedative. The pharmacist knew me and told me not to take it regularly and not in large quantities. I told him not to worry, that I just wanted to sleep a few hours. The sedative went to work, and I found myself woozy, and then slept a long time. If I got up from the bed to go to the bathroom, I'd quickly return, yawning and escaping into sleep. The pills made me go limp, and my body felt heavy and my movements slow. But it was necessary to avoid a breakdown.

Then that was it—it was settled. One morning I got dressed and looked in the mirror. I was like a ghost, but it didn't matter. I walked to the bus station and took the bus to Ismailiya. As soon as I sat down, I felt relieved. Even if I were going to my death, it was more tolerable than my suffering. I slept the whole way, and when the bus reached Ismailiya, it was midnight. I sat in the station café until the provincial buses started running. I felt severed from myself, guided by remote control from some unknown location. I reached Zagazig in the morning rush. The station square was bustling like Tanta squares, but here the streets were broader and the remains of a canal still bisected the city. I asked about the school and stood in front of it at a distance on the pavement. I didn't know if I'd see Tahani or not, but the trip was necessary.

I stood in the summer sun for two hours. I wandered around the school wall, which was whitewashed and covered with ads for infertility treatment and gyms, for opticians and doctors' clinics, and then I'd return to stand at a remove, on the other side of the road. I imagined every woman to be Tahani, but as soon as she drew nearer, the hope evaporated. They were the heaviest two hours of my life. The tension played havoc with my nerves. My hope faded every instant, only to be reborn every instant. I considered phoning her sister, but was too scared and returned to my spot.

It was eleven o'clock and the sun set the air on fire. I spotted Tahani. She was thin. More than three weeks had passed since we said goodbye and she couldn't have changed so much. I almost didn't recognize her. She was haggard and wearing black. I found myself propelled toward her, not thinking about what could happen. Seeing me, her eyes and mouth opened wide. At first, her features took on a look of surprise, which became shock, then fear, and then anger. The anger fixed itself as her final expression.

"You're going to get me killed!" she said with a venom that stopped me in my tracks. "Get out of here."

Then she continued walking purposefully, trying to control her confused steps on the way to the school gate. The malice in her voice and the way she looked at me nailed me to the spot. This isn't Tahani, I thought, but it was. She was like another woman. How could a person conceal a thousand people within? Her panicked face, the malice and venom, split open a chasm of pain that yawned and swallowed me. I kept thinking: That wasn't Tahani, it was another woman who was liable to kill me if I came any closer, just to preserve a miserable life. It seemed I'd been standing in the street forever. Was the earth really shaking or was it my trembling steps? I didn't care to figure it out. It was grueling, what I saw in Tahani's face. How could a person change like that? I didn't actually know where I was going. I could no longer see anything. I was lost.

That was another of my black days. I was stuck in my spot, in my moment. I had no other place or time. I couldn't go back to al-Tur, with its grimness, its cramped confines, and its suffocating air, and I couldn't go back to Tanta, where Janette was waiting for me with her woes and hatred. There was nowhere for me, yet again, and this time it was crueler. Tahani's venomous face cleaved my soul with a knife. Deliverance came when I felt I might collapse and die like my mother in the street. At that moment, the face of my sister Nadia appeared and I pulled myself together. Thank the Lord I was able, in the midst of that delirium, to stop a taxi to take me to the Cairo bus stop and reach my sister's house in Abbasiya before nightfall.

Nadia gasped when she saw me.

"What is it, brother? What's wrong, Yusuf?" she said, and hugged me. I couldn't stop myself from crying like a child, heavy, hot tears that contained everything that had been long pent up in my heart. For the first time, I understood the story of the prodigal son. Everything around me was precious: the cramped apartment, Nadia looking into my face, the maternal compassion radiating from her eyes the way it did from my mother's, the feeling of being in a home.

Nadia was shocked at my appearance and my sobbing. Every time I tried to stop crying, a glance or a scent would send me back again. Everything around me drove me to tears: the bulky living-room furniture, the daylight fading on the balcony, the living-room chairs, Nadia barking at her children telling them to go to their room—"Your uncle's not well"— the smell of cooking that filled the house. It was like I had longed for homes, for a dining-room table and mealtimes. I had a strong urge to see Fadi and Michel, to sleep in my bed, and hear the hiss of the gas heater in winter.

I closed my eyes and sleep carried me away. Nadia touched my shoulder, and I opened my eyes to her smiling face and her thick blond hair.

"I prepared a bath for you," she said.

I walked like I was hypnotized. I took a bath and slept through to the morning. I was almost driven to sobs again when her husband welcomed me, affably scolding me for not visiting them for so long. Sleep had given me some control, and I closed the door on the tears.

We ate breakfast together, and then he went to work and I stayed with my sister. Nadia tried to broach the subject, but I silenced her.

"You're the reason," I joked. "If I hadn't married your friend, I wouldn't be living this miserable life."

"Yusuf, believe me, if you scoured the world, you couldn't find better than Janette. She loves you and wants you, but you're a wanderer. You want to live however you please."

I knew she visited Janette regularly. She reassured me and respected my wish for silence, and she didn't again bring up the scandals I created everywhere.

I left my sister's house and went back to al-Tur, packed my bag, and returned to Tanta.

# Yusuf Tadrus says:

I LEFT TANTA IN SCANDAL and returned in scandal. Scandal pursued me wherever I alighted until I wanted to disappear. I was truly worn out. Feeling that life was a maze, I vented my anger against myself. From the very first days in Tanta, I realized the miseries I'd have to endure. I'd been living the good life in al-Tur, and now it was Janette's turn to torment me. I tried to find excuses for her, thinking that I'd wounded her in a way no woman could tolerate, but my anger only let me see her as the cause of my life's problems. If I hadn't married her, this wouldn't have happened to me. For her part, she thought she had to do me in, because there was no hope that I'd be hers. It was on this toxic foundation that I built my life after my return from al-Tur.

Every morning I'd go to work, crossing al-Hikma Street. As you know, by then the city was teeming with humanity. You couldn't find a place to put your foot, like the world was a necklace that had become unstrung. They installed sewage networks and electrical and telephone lines, paved them over, then dug them up again. You'd run into all manner of vehicle—taxis, horse carts, microbuses, pickup trucks, and city buses. The area hadn't been booming like this when I went to al-Tur, or else my memory was betraying me. It even seemed the heavens were more expansive.

Can you believe we used to complain of what the infitah, liberalization, had done in the 1980s? We didn't know worse was coming. The astounding thing was that people didn't notice the mantle of grime that enveloped us. The farmer women would sit on the side of the road in front of their baskets of vegetables, unaware of the dust accumulating on their faces. Heaps of trash piled up on the corners, the cats frolicking on them. All of that happened around us, was part of us—we were the ones who made it. Every morning the bustle would evoke the days of the alley, kindling a nostalgia for that period as fine as the dust of the road, and that distant time seemed as pure as a dream.

I spent most of the time sitting on the balcony. I thought about taking up cigarettes, but I hated them from the first puff. What exactly do you want, son of Tadrus, I constantly asked myself. Where did this open chasm in you come from and what does it mean? What do you want? You have no hope of getting Tahani. It's over, a fleeting dream. What exactly do you want? Think before you perish.

I started listening to music. As I followed the melodies in my head, they would creep into my heart, but sometimes they hummed in my bones and made me tenser. I listened to Beethoven and Mozart from tapes Rida Boulos had given me. I'd meet him on Friday on his visit to Tanta.

"Don't worry, Yusuf," he told me on the last visit. "It's a difficult period that'll pass."

We met at a downtown café or, if he were pressed for time, he'd ask me to come to his grandmother's house. He'd often repeat, "Painting is the way, Yusuf." I saw it as flattery or just a speech tic. The last time I'd looked at him baffled, like he was speaking of someone else. I couldn't understand him. He had more insight into me than I did myself, believed more in my abilities. He understood life. But I was living in muck I couldn't extricate myself from.

The house was hell. Janette never stopped moving in the apartment, aggrieved and angry, and always asking me to help her with something: install a faucet, unclog a drain, hammer a nail into the wall. Her demands were unceasing. She wanted to entangle and embed me in her life any way she could. She couldn't just let me be. She had to perturb my life just for the sake of it. She'd talk about household expenses, the money never quite enough though we had a reasonable life, and would toss off comments about me sitting on the balcony listening to music while people were working second shifts to provide a better life for their children. The strange thing is, if I'd thought about working more, she would have objected and demanded I stay where I was so she could enact her revenge.

Janette didn't know me and she wouldn't know me until she accepted her situation and knew with certainty that she could not grasp me in her clutches. I was already in the grasp of forces greater than her: fantasies and figures and a totally different inner awareness. She wouldn't abandon these maneuvers until she was exhausted and weary and finally started sympathizing with this troubled man.

In the months that followed my return from al-Tur, her thirst for vengeance was mighty. I accepted it as part of the dust cloud that encased our life, realizing the measure of her injury. Sana was easier, but Tahani was a deep wound that made her determined to destroy me. I didn't appreciate that she loved me and that she was a woman, too.

My psychological troubles began. I went to Zagazig a few times and stood like a vagrant in front of Tahani's school, circling it and wandering the streets. There, behind those walls, an irretrievable ecstasy flickered. I'd find myself in a funk returning from school, lost and hopeless and hating everything around me—the house, the school, the streets, the people—so I'd head for the station and take the train to Zagazig. And I'd feel a living breath of air in my spirit, a hope that I knew at the outset was empty, but it was still a ghost of a hope. I'd wander the streets, sit in cafés, and stay there until night.

Upon my return, Janette would ask me about my absence. I'd sit silently, struck dumb for several days, as if transfixed. Where had the light I'd seen for a few moments in Tahani's arms gone? How could I recapture that paradise? I wasn't able to see Tahani again, but I would go back to her city as if drawing nearer to her and relive the details of that week, which I considered the most precious I had experienced. Strangely, I'd erased the venom from her face as if it had never been, as if it were the face of someone else. I stopped at the moment she got into the car at the al-Tur bus stop.

Michel's need for English lessons saved me from the inferno. It wouldn't do for him to take lessons when his father was an English teacher. I began tutoring him, forcing myself to do it, and little by little I started to ask about his life and we began talking about his friends and his troubles. His tale was a retelling of the story of persecution generation after generation. It saddens the heart. Maybe one day this sorrow will come to an end, but even today it remains a cross, borne by one generation after the other, until that time comes, if it comes.

Michel's struggle was the opposite of his brother's. Fadi was an animal from the day he was born, a terrible force and a wholly physical being. Since his early years in primary school, he'd come home with a scraped face. Not a day passed without a fight. Where did he get the vigor? Maybe from his grandfather Tadrus, maybe from Janette's rebellious spirit. I watched him in wonder. In the summer vacation, instead of sitting at home, he'd go to the jewelers' district, gold-plating metal at his uncle Nagib's workshop. He was an irreverent joker, constantly pestering his mother. Maybe he deflected some of her hostility from me. Michel, though, was morose, focused even at that early age on "getting away from here." That was the mantra around which his life revolved as he was growing up, until he made good on it after graduating from the College of Tourism and Hotel Management.

My psychological distress grew. The fears I've spoken to you about found fertile ground in that period. I imagined Janette wanted to get rid of me. My anxieties began to get the upper hand. Where did such notions come from? Did I wake up one day to find her standing next to the bed holding a knife? Or was it a dream? I was obsessed with the idea that she would poison me. I'd tell myself: You're crazy, Yusuf, we're all eating the same food and she couldn't poison her own children. I was certain Janette could not do that. Despite all the rancor, I felt her love, though it was a mirror image, reflected as an urge to destroy. But how can you persuade paranoid whispers with rational argument? I'd jokingly tell myself that Janette couldn't do it because if she got rid of me, she'd have no one to vent her resentment at. None of this quelled the anxieties. Ironically, I shortly learned that the person who wanted to do Yusuf Tadrus in was none other than Yusuf Tadrus.

Things went from bad to worse when Mr. Naim made a reappearance, seeking to rectify my relationship with the church that had been ruined by my recklessness. One day he passed by my school and asked if we could meet at the Mari Girgis Church on Sunday evening. I knew that he served as a lay pastor at the church for civil servants, or something like that. It was voluntary, a role in which he could find himself and ultimately help people. Gradually, a grudge built inside me toward him and his role. I saw that, in a subtle way, he contributed to the insularity, helping to separate us from those we lived with.

"Your relative wants to see me," I told Rida Boulos on Friday when I saw him.

"Yusuf, don't be so touchy and listen. He's a good man, really; he only wants the best for you."

I went to meet with Mr. Naim on Sunday. The few visitors were on their way out. I love church courtyards. There's a kind of serenity, especially after mass. There's expectation and an openness to life, a kindness looming in people's faces, tranquility and optimism. I was wearing a short-sleeved shirt and the cool air sent a chill through my body. I had lost a lot of weight. I didn't eat well, my nerves were shot, and I became

159

aware of an anger building inside like steam under pressure. And then here came Mr. Naim to teach me how to live.

I stood at the church door looking at the faces of the young girls and boys, thinking of what I used to do when I would come here with my mother. I heard Mr. Naim's voice calling me. He was sitting on a wooden bench in the outer courtyard.

"Come sit next to me," he said.

After some moments of silence, I heard him clear his throat and start to speak. As usual, he walked around the topic, talking first about the temptations of life, the caprices of youth, and the confused soul who finds his salvation only in the bosom of the Lord. Then he began talking about me, also edging in on the subject, starting from my mother and talking about her pure life and how people esteemed her and remembered her sacrifices and indefatigable work at the association. Finally, he broached the matter at hand.

"Surely a person must find himself weary of caprice and long for right living and repentance." Then he said offhandedly that he had asked to meet me there to discuss my life.

I listened to him apprehensively, and when he said "my life" so casually, I tensed up. I almost got up and left, but I remembered Rida telling me to listen and learn. I sat there grudgingly, irritated at the way he spoke and the way he gave himself the right to interfere in people's lives.

I could never understand it, even though friends and relatives indulged it and thought Mr. Naim a good person who helped people out of love of the Lord. I didn't want to finish the conversation. I knew myself, knew I'd lose my temper with him. I held my tongue and listened. The gist of his words, spoken in that roundabout way of his, was that I was a wayward son and the time had come to return to the fold. That's not how I felt, though. He didn't understand—I didn't want to discuss the story of the prodigal son, and he wasn't a confessor, and as he continued to talk, I could no longer stand the interference and the way he talked about me as if I weren't there. When he asked me bluntly when my last confession was, I glared at him and spoke my mind. I don't know why I bore such hatred for the man. He hadn't harmed me. In fact, he had done his best to rescue me and spare me further trouble.

Losing my temper, I informed him that I wasn't a prodigal son. I was right with the Lord and knew in my heart that He forgave me. But I was no longer right with Yusuf.

"Do you have a way I can make my peace with him?" I taunted.

He responded kindly, "So then, you have not made peace with the Lord."

"Yusuf Tadrus is not the Lord, so that making it right with him means making it right with the Lord," I continued, heedless of everything. "You don't get it. My relationship with the Lord is very personal, here in my heart. Why are you interfering with it? You're not a confessor. I feel the Lord in my heart and when He's angry with me, I know it. I also know when He's pleased with me. He's the one who led me into this maze and He's watching me from up there, to see how I'll get out or if I'll rot and lose my way and keel over. Every day I'm uncertain and confused. I don't know when He will open my eyes and guide me to the path. These prepackaged formulas for guidance don't work for a corrupt soul, the soul of someone like me, believe me, Mr. Naim. Believe your young charge and don't bother yourself with me."

I left him sitting there and walked the streets, confused, not knowing where to go. Every time I considered returning home in such a rage I was afraid. Maybe I'd lose my temper and take it out on Janette or the boys. I was miserable and confused, and again had the urge to cry.

I met Rida Boulos on Friday.

"Tell your relative to let me be," I told him. "I'm not a miscreant for him to think he can earn some reward by bringing me back to the fold. I'm not an errant child. I'm lost, I don't know my way, and that's it. And I don't know if I'll reach the end or if it will continue like this."

Rida smiled. He'd finished shaving and had put on his jacket.

"The man respects you. He doesn't want to see you adrift."

I laughed. "Well, do me a favor and tell him not to treat me like that. I've started to dread him—he only pops up in my life when disaster strikes."

The years raced by like that, as the boys grew up and took more and more attention. Like I said, maybe it was my relationship with the kids that pierced a hole in my prison and, with time, I also started noticing Janette's sorrows. She had high blood pressure, and sometimes she went into her room, closed the door, and cried.

At Christmas, Nadia visited with her kids. She stayed a few days and I took a break from Janette's drudgery as she again laughed with Nadia, remembering their school days and the years of fun. They went out together to buy holiday things, and we visited relatives, and I started feeling a need for holidays and companionship. I was fed up with exile. It was in that period that I saw Janette again. I started noticing her sweet laugh and her dimples. On the last day I took Nadia and her children to the station.

"Shame on you, Yusuf," she said sadly. "You've wronged Janette. She never loved anyone but you, and her whole life she's wanted to please you."

Maybe calm returned to my life after that. I don't remember how it happened, but with time, things became settled at home. Before Easter, Nadia called and made me promise to come spend the holiday in Cairo with Janette and the boys. I hadn't traveled with my family in a long time, and you know the details of family life stress me out. I told Nadia her brother wasn't well: his nerves were frazzled, and he couldn't tolerate it.

"We'll leave you alone," she said. "Go downtown and meet your friends. Go to museums and art galleries."

See? No one would forget Yusuf the painter, except Yusuf himself. Secretly, they were all waiting for Yusuf to create paintings the likes of which had never been seen.

We left on Thursday and reached my sister's at night. The kids all went out together while we sat visiting late into the night. Again I felt closer to Janette, remembering how lovely she was. Yes, she had filled out some, but her cheerfulness showed, as if she'd grown tired of being miserable. On Friday I left them to wander around Muizz Street, and the next day I went to the churches in Old Cairo. I couldn't escape the outing on Shamm al-Nisim and went with them to the zoo, sitting there peacefully. They all imagined that things had finally settled down, but to be honest, something was missing.

I won't deny that every year I'd apply to proctor the matriculation exams in some distant place. Maybe I'd run into Tahani. When exam time came, my heart trembled and lurched, a mixture of anxiety and anticipation. But as the years passed, I began to fear I'd find Tahani and again demolish the fragile edifice I'd rebuilt. After the age of forty, I no longer wanted to demolish. I was no longer capable of that kind of impetuosity and wished my heart would stop seeking such impulses. I imagined I was worn out and that that was it—there was nothing else left. My elder son was grown, his Adam's apple sprouted, and my soul had become as black and stagnant as brackish water.

It was then that I began to think about entering the monastic life and leaving everything behind, as if the resurrection dream would be fulfilled in spite of me. My whole life, the idea had been unthinkable, but the weariness of that period, the inertia, convinced me of its merits: nothing could fill the void inside except God. I started dreaming often of the resurrection rite in different guises. As in former days, it seemed to be a prophecy, and in that period it became a summons, but every time I ventured closer to the idea, I shrank back. At other moments, it seemed my only solution. All roads were closed and I would never heal.

# Yusuf Tadrus says:

EVERY TIME YOU FEEL YOUR life has been anchored in place, a moment comes that carries you elsewhere. Then you know that life doesn't stop and that as long as you have one breath left, some energy will continue to seek an outlet. I'd settled down and said that's it, all that's left is a series of indistinguishable days I'll pass through like a sleepwalker. The idea of the monastery would resolve itself in time. But there is some energy under the skin, unknown until it rises up demanding release. That's what I learned in those years that flew by, the days so alike I can find no tale to tell about them save the boys moving from class to class, until Michel was taking the matriculation exams and Fadi was in middle school. There is nothing there save tiny details, minutiae you need a microscope to see. An empty life whose most important element was my own fraught relationship with myself.

Long ago, I'd stopped looking in the mirror, as if I wanted to blot out the memory of my face. Maybe that was the source of the urge for a monastic life. I wanted to forget my face, but it never forgot me, not ever. I was reminded of it by the way women were drawn to me and the way they talked to me. I started to feel this face had nothing to do with me. When an English teacher came to the school, a young, freshly graduated woman who was drawn to me, I quickly bolted. I no longer had the energy for such adventures. A deep certainty took root that this face had become a mask, a façade unrelated to the person I was.

Have you tried it? Tried looking in the mirror and asking yourself who that is? Have you experienced that contradiction between your sense of self and your sense of your face? Your face is not simply a collection of features, you know. It's the key to life events. You find yourself standing in line to pay the phone bill, and the woman at the counter smiles at you and picks you out of the line to help you first without waiting. And you have nothing to offer but a smile and a promise to one day return the favor. The way you look is not simply features affixed to your face. It's a living thing that affects your life. It reflects a certain image of you, and you come to know it through people's impressions, demonstrated in the way they act with you. And when the two images conflict, it is deeply disorienting. Why are they acting like that? Why do they single me out for hostility or love at first sight? I'm not the person whose face they see. The confusion persists: Who am I? The thorny question that has remained humanity's problem since the dawn of consciousness. It's difficult, the barrier between yourself and the being who inhabits your body.

Don't look at me like I'm from another planet. I'm from here, from the same climate you came from. I bet you've been through similar moments. Maybe you didn't notice them; maybe someone else noticed them even more profoundly than I did. Don't be deceived by the preoccupation with life affairs. It's more like fleeing the peering inner eye, the eye that follows a person from birth to death. Everyone wants to blind it—to be rid of that irritating internal surveillance—but I was ensnared. I stared into the eye, or it stared into me, and that's what happened.

In any case, evils are not pure evil. Even the desire to be rid of yourself is a step toward your emancipation. Like I said, in this period my life sank to the depths of its stagnancy. The idea of monasticism loomed very close, and I secretly began preparing myself for it. I went to the church and asked Father Bula to suggest someone to mentor me and show me how to prepare myself. I started reading the Bible with a punishing regularity. Until that unanticipated transformation.

I met Bilal al-Sheikh at the school and the tide turned. How did it happen? How to explain it? Don't ask me. I know now it was coincidence that saved me. Maybe it was my mother's prayers, I don't know, but the monastery preparations ceased instantaneously and vanished.

I was at school one day and heard a voice call out to me: "Yusuf! Yusuf Tadrus!" The voice was familiar. I knew who it belonged to but couldn't place it. I looked behind me, toward the principal's office, and saw a bald man, so fat his chin covered his neck. He was looking at me with familiarity and in an instant I knew it was Bilal al-Sheikh. I hadn't seen him since I'd torn up the paintings after leaving his house. That was a long time ago. A lifetime.

Backtracking, I went down the stairs, stunned that this man was the same person who wrote the *Manifesto of May 30*. "For the eye to be a sun, the heart a sun, the spirit a sun." I approached him, greeting him warmly with the same old fraternal affection and asking how he was. He had become an art faculty supervisor after his return from a secondment in the Emirates. We sat and talked awhile. I asked him about Hazim al-Shirbini. He said he'd returned from Algeria and now worked at the Palace of Culture. Hussein now lived in Cairo and wrote articles about art and television for an evening paper. I walked him out of the school and to his car, listening to him dumbfounded. Nothing had changed. He spoke in the same old way, retrieving scripts from the musty archive and reading them to me as if I'd never heard them.

On edge, I returned to the school. I hadn't expected to ever run into anyone from the Ankh Society. Even with my old comrades, Muhammad and Karim, I had only a passing relationship. I met Muhammad once rushing out of the train station, coming to the city for a quick visit to his mother. He taught at the Faculty of Humanities in Cairo. He was preparing his doctoral thesis and occasionally wrote in the Friday *al-Ahram*. Karim no longer had any ties to painting. He'd graduated from the College of Business and worked with his father in the auto parts trade. He'd become wholly caught up in his life. I'd see him sometimes when Rida Boulos needed a spare part and we would remember the days at the studio at the Palace of Culture and laugh at our naïveté. But still Karim would wax nostalgic, saying, "My God, Yusuf, those were the days!"

Karim's appearance, the way he talked, and the sight of him in the middle of the auto-parts shop erased any memory of him at the Palace of Culture, so I didn't consider him part of the past and seeing him didn't have the same impact. But Bilal al-Sheikh's abrupt appearance was disorienting, stirring ambivalent feelings tinged with anger. For the past to be resurrected so suddenly—it was like it was sticking its tongue out at me, showing me that I was still attached to those values I'd absorbed in my youth; that they'd been hiding the whole time beneath my stagnant life. It exposed my naïve daydreams, demonstrating, too, that I was still drawn to painting despite my silence and distance and immersion in my life.

Imagine, I had been unconsciously (though acutely) aware of painting, waiting for it to rear its head and find me. I had been leaning on the residue of innocence and light left from the Ankh Society evenings, and now here was the sheikh of the society coming to make a mockery of this secret attachment.

Like I told you, I had a bad relationship with myself. Meeting Bilal dredged up an unexpected degree of self-loathing and bitterness at the naïveté of my attachment to pointless things.

I went to my class and gave the kids an exercise to copy into their notebooks. Wound up, and having imposed silence on the students, I paced the classroom and thought. So *that's* how it is, these are the suns, the lodestars, for our lives: return from the Emirates, buy an apartment in a tower on al-Nadi

Street, drive a car, get the boy into the military college, and look for a perfect husband for the girl. Precisely the easy life Bilal used to ridicule. All these lodestars, then, were just the inability to live the easy life, and when you finally were able to live it, the stars went black, persisting only as an ornament, a conversational embellishment. So that's how it is, then?

I returned home that day feeling betrayed. It was a distant, hollow sense of failure, because it exposed my hidden attachment to painting and the brittleness of what I'd experienced in that period as life. Life should be solid. You're supposed to be certain of it and live it like it's reality. But when it suddenly shows itself as merely a cover for the secret urge to paint—well, that can lead you to damnation.

I was furious with myself. Were all those ideas that shone in our youth lies? Naïve things that would never be realized? I was furious that Bilal had not made good on those old words, and it turned those old hopes into pipe dreams. Maybe I was waiting for that encounter to crack open an awareness of the rage buried in me. What a waste, the frivolity of everything! The frivolity of my entire life. It was all for naught and I was nothing, and what had so swept me up in life was fantasy upon fantasy. My self-hatred stretched to its outer limits. I wanted to open up a wound and rub salt in it.

Ironically, the encounter sent me back to painting. I found myself at day's end preparing the oils and placing a mirror on the wall at eye level, and then I started painting that fantasy named Yusuf Tadrus. I'll paint the nine faces of Yusuf Tadrus, I told myself mockingly, and then I decided to paint ninety-nine self-portraits. I began in anger and with a desire for something I didn't fathom. Painting ninety-nine self-portraits is a massive undertaking that could take years. A few days later, I was hooked.

The first portrait showed a rusty hand and shaky proportions, painting still out of reach. Painting is like playing the piano; it requires constant exercise of the fingers.

My return to painting delighted Michel, who hadn't known that side of me except through a few old paintings Janette had stored behind the wardrobe. When Fadi came back from his lesson, he gave it a cocky look and said, "What, are you *painting*?" But after a few days, they were increasingly drawn to the paintings, which started showing improvement, and another view of their father began to appear on their faces: a look of amazement at this creature who lived among them.

Life itself is madness. An ordinary thing—something everyone around you accepts as ordinary—can seem utterly mad in retrospect. Why did my return to painting start with self-portraits? Explain that. Help me understand, because I truly do not. Why did I launch that war on my features? Was it my face that was the problem? Why did I wage such a long struggle with myself?

The first portraits were naïve, painted by someone without a grasp of lines, and with gross errors in proportions. As work continued, I could produce just the face there on my identification card. Later, the portraits started coming in spurts, reflecting some deeper aspect of my being. Sometimes the portrait would be dominated by a single impression, like the day I painted the lantern, or the day I was locked up in the workshop at the Holy Bible Association, or the day I waited at the door of the morgue in the al-Minshawi Hospital.

I threw myself into it and it gripped me, giving me a different feeling about my life. I thought I'd make some charcoal sketches, and I spent a long time scouring the lines of the face and its shifts. I didn't know myself. I had been floating on the surface, and now I started contemplating the being I lived in. The eye had a disguised sadness; the press of the lips a childish indignation, self-regard and arrogance; in their fullness a lasciviousness. The heart was open there. Could one get at something by painting those pictures? Why was I so enamored of painting my own visage? The best thing about the experience was the boys' connection with me, the way every day they asked me what number I'd reached. They were waiting for the ninety-ninth portrait. Life changed, a little, as Janette watched from a distance in wary silence. Things had calmed down, but the sudden gust of painting made her uneasy, and she viewed my efforts with suspicion.

The project evolved and I painted the face in peculiar ways, playing with the features. I painted elongated eyebrows, coarse, full lips—agape, pressed together, and slack—and bulging eyes. I caricatured the features in several paintings and then moved on to painting the face as it appeared in my interior eye. I took down the mirror and painted from my head. The faces I painted, which resembled me in some way, led me to fantastic misshapen figures. "Horror pictures," Michel said one day. An interior terror crept into the canvas, giving rise to monstrous creatures with the faces of animals. The disfigurement wasn't like the physical deformity in Egon Schiele's paintings. It was the warped sensibility of fairy tales, like the pictures of imps and demons. But that soon passed, when I painted a face looking out a train window, tortured and melancholy, the disfigurement coming from the inner pain.

I started to understand a bit. I had to paint the expressions of the face reflected in the mirror. I got the mirror again. I left the expressions free to mutate, a mixture of the image in the mirror and an image seen through a murky glass or overtaken by mist—distant, dark faces with undetermined features. The boys forgot about the number of paintings when I entered that phase of uncertainty.

I was slowly divorcing myself from my life. I did my job like a ghost. I was unwittingly distancing myself. The faces I saw in the street began to shift, replaced by my own features. I affixed my features to every face I saw and then marveled: the image is the same. The human being is a single creature with different features. I regained my skill at portraiture in that period, and came to fear staring into people's faces. I again felt the power of the gaze to penetrate. I was chasing some unknown phantom.

Was the experience a ritualistic purging of the self? What is the self that peers out behind the face? What does it want? Who is that being looking out at me? Could I know it? Was there really a "self" separate from the face? The face kept company with me and played with me. It looked upon me, smiling, and then mutated. I would leave a painting for a few minutes to go to the bathroom or go to the kitchen to make a cup of coffee, and when I returned I'd find it had transformed. The features had assumed another expression, the self had another question, maybe lust, bereavement, or bafflement at this insanity.

The portraits at times seemed to be a contemplation of long-ago moments. The eye was that of a child holding his mother's hand or looking at the light in awe. Then my mother came and started to insinuate herself into the portraits, imprinting her features on mine. I tried to be rid of it, saying I'd faithfully paint the face apparent in the mirror, but my mother continued to hover in the features. I only discovered how much my face resembled hers when I painted it. A full-on Oedipal complex. Your psychoanalyst friends would see it more clearly than you or I. My mother inhabited the eyes and lips, and maybe the yearning for God.

The resemblance frightened me a little, but then I yielded and accepted the Oedipal complex. I started painting my features with the aim of bringing out her likeness, but they played a trick on me and my uncle Murad appeared, then my uncle Nasim and my mother's entire family. Features began inserting themselves into ever more distant portraits until they no longer resembled me. I was playing, developing something I didn't see then. It was strange to see my ancestors looking out at me in my own portrait, having a reunion in my features. At the end, I sat there marveling at my discovery that I was no more than the tale of a woman who loved God.

I'm a troublemaker—that's the overall gist of me. But I actually experienced moments of magic and pure joy seeing the masks slip off one after another. Yusuf the good guy, the villain, the narcissist, the bohemian, and the lecher. Yusuf the coward, the negligent, the unlucky, the wretch, the womanizer. The one who conceals things in clefts in the wall, the morose, the self-pitying. The Yusuf who wants to run to his mother so she can pat him on the shoulder and tell him, "You're my son, my only one."

It's a strange experience, to stumble on a sense of comprehension and human complexity. Personal discoveries give you insight into yourself and your situation in life. The most important thing that happened to me was observing the shift and multiplicity of the "I," but it was simultaneously nerve-racking and torturous. I'd pause at a particular expression and say: That's it, that's it, I've captured the feeling that represents me. I'd keep at it for a few days, painting the portrait that I thought carried the collected personality, but then it would mutate, representing just one shifting aspect of me.

It's the nature of portraiture that the image represents a single impression, one instant of the thousands that pass over the features. I was in an impossible attempt. Was I searching for the unachievable? A portrait to convey the unadulterated soul, the permanence behind the shifting, primal spirit living behind the walls, hidden under the details? The authentic feeling. It was all fantasy on top of fantasy. And then the portrait I was searching for came to me accidentally.

I'd grown tired. I had spent I don't know how many months carving out snatches of time to go to work, do household errands, and keep up with Michel's lessons. Fadi tried to make it easier for me—"Don't worry yourself about me," he'd say archly; "I can handle myself"—but Janette was getting more bellicose. Really, how could anyone tolerate such madness? I understood it then. Janette was the one who stopped me from going mad. It was she who preserved whatever

173

self-possession I had left. If I were alone, I would have long ago wigged out, as the kids say now.

It was a few days before the boys' exams, a summer night. I was confused and depleted. I'd prepared a canvas to paint on, an old painting that bore the traces of failed portraits. I painted it black and thought I'd give it a try. Painting is expensive, as you know, and I'm poor. I've got to use my materials wisely. I sat staring at the black for a long time, and then reached for the brush. I started painting lines of the face from memory, in white, the basic strokes I knew by heart. I nearly placed a light stroke after finishing the skull, to gesture to the eye, but then pulled back. The blackness of the painting wasn't total. The previous paintings on the same canvas gave the color a contrast in several spots and specters danced there behind the black color. I looked closely. My image was there, looking out from within the black, framed by the white lines. There was no need to paint the features. I thought I was hallucinating. Could simply carefully drawing the lines of the skull produce my visage like this? I sat on the couch, looking at the portrait in awe. It was hard, what with the weariness and tension. I closed my eyes and opened them. My image was now clearer within the lines I'd painted. It was a moment of terror. A complete portrait looked out from the heart of the blackness without my having to paint the features.

That was the most amazing moment in my journey. There was only the white line framing the face and yet it was the most perfect expression of something that had escaped me. A dark void: that was Yusuf Tadrus. It was exactly that. I sat staring at the frame for two hours. Every time I looked, my image shifted, but it remained the features of Yusuf Tadrus. The ninety-nine portraits were all there in that empty frame of a human face. That inky depth expressed the soul with an eloquence gifted by chance, poverty, and the scarcity of supplies. I went to the balcony and closed my eyes. Then I went to the bathroom, telling myself it was all in my head. But coming back to the portrait,

I'd find it an exact representation of me: the incomplete round-ness of the skull, the pointy chin, the slight forward slant.

The faint dawn light started coming in through the bal-cony. I heard movement in the living room and saw Fadi on his way to the bathroom. I couldn't contain myself: I called him and stood him in front of the portrait.

"What do you see?" I asked. "Your picture, Dad." He looked at me, befuddled. "Dude, let me sleep."

I grabbed him by the arm, afraid he'd leave without understanding it. "How did you know?" I asked.

He looked at me again, puzzled. "It's just you."

That's what I was striving for the whole time unawares. All those past months, I had been struggling to create that portrait. So what did it mean, you say. Maybe nothing. I'm talking to figure it out and you ask me? Look, I don't intend to show that portrait. Rida Boulos begged to buy it, but I refused. I won't let it go. It has no value for anyone else—it carries a message for me.

I couldn't leave the living room. I didn't go to work. I lay on the couch with the portrait in front of me. The next day I went to work, and as soon as I returned to the house, I headed for the living room and stood in front of the portrait. The strength of its presence persisted day after day. It became even more powerful. One day when I returned from school and entered the living room to look at it, I found its lips smiling at me from within, a bemused look mocking my situation and my brittle, empty existence. The portrait was addressing me, talking to me. I knew it might possess me and spirit away my mind.

They're true, those folktales that warn children about staring too long into the mirror lest they go crazy. Mirrors can bewitch you. Staring at yourself for such a long time can deaden your sense of the world around you. This obsession with the self-portrait, as if I were searching for something unknown to me, made me ill. I started talking to myself, until Janette pulled me back from the dark, agonizing search for absurdity. She stopped me as I came back from outside and touched off a fight because I'd forgotten to buy the things she'd asked for.

The reason for the fight was that there was no bread in the house. Michel or Fadi could have gone out and it would be done, but it was too late for that. The painting experiment had rekindled her resentment. She'd married a madman, she said as she gathered up her clothes, and she was going to live at her brother's so she didn't go mad too. She left the house that night. It was the first night she'd ever spent outside her home.

Clarity arrived. I sat in the living room, the television playing for itself, as I became cognizant of my state. Wake up, Yusuf pal, I said. Michel and Fadi were in their room, silent, and there was no sound in the apartment save the television, as if the house were abandoned. I stayed in my spot for hours, feeling the emptiness around me, stretching out without end.

The next evening, Nagib came, this time without Mr. Naim, but with Father Bula in tow. We spoke calmly, and Father Bula said that life is adversity and we must help ourselves make it through. Michel was about to matriculate, and there were household expenses and costly private lessons. I had to look for a second job after work. Janette was tired of scrimping and saving and cooperatives. I had to shoulder part of the load with her. I couldn't let her carry the worry while I sat around painting my face without interruption.

I saw how far I had gone, compelled to follow my features and forgetting everything else. It was like I wanted to reach the root of the features to expunge them. It was an absurd experiment, no doubt, from which that crisis pulled me back. I *was* kind of mad.

Father Bula suggested I tutor students at the church and work with Nagi Fahim in the art-supply shop—he needed a painter. And so another journey began.

It's dizzying. A person could have been broken along the way or lost, never reaching any destination.

# Yusuf Tadrus says:

In a moment resembling madness, when all time and place have no existence, a limpid moment that a gnostic might call ecstasy, or something else, your ordinary consciousness does not function. Another type of figurative consciousness supplants cognition. It's like a heightened perceptive state, an emotionally charged atmosphere, not merely a passing thought. There was revealed to me what was hidden behind the events of my life. I was shown my secret attachment to my own visage, as if I were in love with it. I was fulfilling my mother's love for me without knowing it. People are strange. They reproduce the relationships that originally shaped them and feel about themselves the way people do. Their relationship with the self is a re-articulation of the feelings of those around them, especially in their formative years. Yusuf Tadrus was a shadow. He imagined he had smashed his own personal myth when he was in al-Tur, when he discovered he was destined for nothing, but that was only a brief glimpse of the larger illusion he lived that was exposed during the painting. Painting my self-portrait was central to understanding my own myth, and to understanding that everyone forms his own personal myth.

Listen, I'll tell you what remains in my mind now from that experience. Don't laugh, please, I'm a solitary person unfamiliar with intellectual debates like you. These are just my thoughts—they may be worthless—but let me tell you what happened within me then. It occurred to me that every human being thinks himself a god. Even if I wasn't sure of it, I had at least lived thinking myself a god. With that experience, I understood my myth. Then there appeared the many experiences of people I'd known who formed their own personal myths about themselves, most obviously the Ankh Society. Then I thought that many people's lives are based on a fiction they nurture or that unwittingly takes shape in their selves, on which the rest of their life is based. It's a kind of fiction formed through their relationship with their mother or father or friends, or their social status, like with presidents and kings, officers, judges, and doctors. And also with religious leaders—all of them believe in their depths that they're executing God's word on earth. They commune with God, in other words. Some divine touch in their beings elevates them above the rest of humanity, and when you meet one of them, they treat you like a wayward son, like they possess the absolute truth. Those who possess absolute power and an absolute truth partake of divinity, and therein lies the catastrophe.

Anyway, there's a kind of order in the life of every person. Let him take some time to consider his life. In the beginning he'll think his path was drawn entirely by coincidence—his name, religion, and features, his genetic disposition. He can't be disentangled from his constitution, but he did act. He did one thing and not other things, walked down that street and passed the other by, fought with this person and loved that one. He can perceive the connections in that jumbled scrawl that constitutes his life. He sees what his choices wrought and where coincidence led him. This stuff that shaped his life has its own special code, and when a person deciphers it, he discovers a certain meaning, and he sees his myth glittering behind it. Even people who hate their lives and think about suicide— what that does to them is their discovery of their life's code: my life isn't worth living. Isn't that a code, a meaning?

I saw my life's code glittering behind my actions. I saw that inner feeling that I was a unique person, touched by divinity—a feeling implanted by the Sitt Umm Yusuf. Delusions of grandeur, I know. That was my curse. Believe me, I didn't see the light until I saw myself as this puny, fleeting being. I saw life without illusion, without myth, and then I started to live. This deluded sense of self-worth is deeply rooted in the fear of nothingness and a desire in all people for life without limit. Humans want to share immortality with God.

I won't talk about others, just myself. That will no doubt confirm my superiority–persecution complex, but I don't care. It occurs to me that I never saw the earth except when I realized with dismay that I wanted to be a god. Sweet heavens, it's unnerving! It was working below my skin, unbeknownst to me. It was the origin of the monastery idea, and maybe of the resurrection dream, too. It would have been a disaster if I'd gone to the monastery. It truly scares me when I think about it now. If I had gone to the monastery, it would have only solidified the myth, making it a reality. I would have lived in absolute misery, imagining I was cleansing myself of the narrow, paltry human and replacing it with the vastness of the universe, the unbound spirit.

No way. If that had happened, I would've been finished. I really was on the brink of crossing over to the other bank, and that would have been the worst thing to happen to me. I'd be a god in human guise, and that's what I need to be rid of to be able to live, to be able to smell the fresh breeze of the days that remain to me on this earth. If I'd entered the monastery, I would have continued to live with the illusion, deluded that I had made great strides in God's path, fruitlessly chasing the light. Now I feel letting that go was an essential condition for life. For a person to live like a tiller of the soil, knowing he was created like all the creatures around him, knowing he's transitory, but still he plants a tree, because he venerates life, not himself—such a person understands life better than monks and Sufis. It's that understanding that lets him savor the good things in life. You can savor the tea we're drinking now as we listen to Umm Kulthum.

In a different way I savored our forays around the city and the cafés where we sat, our endless talks. You know the small café in the passage near al-Sayyid al-Badawi? The one we sat at yesterday? I stumbled on it. I was walking aimlessly, having painted a cumbersome piece—I couldn't tolerate its intensity—when I spied it hidden behind that mulberry tree. Remember the café next to the Sheikha Sabah Mosque? The old café in the little alleyway that comes out on Said Street? All those cafés mean more to me than anything. All the cups of tea there hold a secret like the secret of prayer. All those conversations, the empty prattle and reflection, the tales—a person can't understand them, can't really savor and experience them, when he's under the spell of the delusion. He has to snap out of it to be able to live the truth of his existence. As long as you're entranced by the hidden spell, you can't see anything. Maybe, if you're lucky enough, circumstances may let you see the light. Or you may never see it.

Look at Amm Saudi there, carrying a tray and heading for the workshop opposite. I watch him every day. I've painted him dozens of times. I haven't been able to give shape to his song and create the mood around him. I'll do it one day: I'll paint him there with his tray on his outstretched palm, so tall he connects earth and sky, around him the small houses. I'll paint him in white and the houses and alleys in dark colors, as if it's nighttime, and there, despite stretching from the earth to the heavens, he'll look just like himself, like Amm Saudi, while in the background Umm Kulthum sings, "You got my eyes used to the sight of you."

# Yusuf Tadrus says:

I CAME BACK FROM THE madness, but the madness lurked, waiting to transform into pictures. I won't deny that the experience was the beginning of salvation, of reaching the shore. Yes, there is exhaustion, but the joy of arrival eases the strain. I was like a person lost at sea who catches sight of a gull and the smell of cities. I understood, learned, and accepted. Acceptance is key here; it's a cognizance and insight into your state and ability and what that means. Most important of all was that the step was taken. This is life. I had to take on my share of its worries, teaching the kids at the church and helping Janette run the house. This share of worry must be borne, otherwise something will be lacking. It wasn't yet clear at that time if I'd actually paint or not. The important thing was I'd returned to it. I had returned to the only thing I'm good for. I reclaimed it, a window through which I could see the side I loved. It was the beginning of the road. Or should we say the end? Either way. *Beginning* and *end* are just words used to contain the incomprehensible.

One day I heard a hard knock on the door. I opened it and found Rida Boulos, again. I'd lost contact with him a while back, and instead of calling, he came in person. He entered the living room, angry I hadn't asked after him.

"You're a hopeless case," he said as he sat on the chair facing the balcony.

Some of the portraits were still behind the chairs, and several were piled up in a corner. Catching sight of them, Rida broke off and spread them out around him on the chairs, in complete silence. He saw what was left of the self-portraits, a portrait from each stage, starting with the identification portrait, and on through the paintings of my mother and ancestors. The final portrait I'd put on top of the wardrobe in the boys' room. He called for Janette and asked for a big glass of tea. Then he examined the paintings for a long time, switching and rearranging some of them. I let him do what he wanted without interfering.

"You and your blasted mind. Look at all these! You made them all out of one picture?"

He was silent again and rearranged the portraits again.

"I told you a long time ago," he continued, "but you didn't believe me."

The various faces on the chairs seemed like old friends I'd known one day, or long-lost relatives, a family living in me that gathered now around Rida Boulos. I was happy he liked the paintings, and I felt some of them showed a measure of skill.

"It's not like you think," I said. "It was more like settling scores."

"So what? Keep at it," he said with the enthusiasm of a businessman; then, leaning back in the chair: "These portraits, they're hard to look at."

"I nearly went crazy."

"And now?"

"I'm okay."

Rida realized the ambivalence of the experience. He understood the state in which I'd painted the portraits, and that's a blessing I'll never cease thanking the Lord for. He gave me a friend capable of understanding me as I am, capable of understanding what everyone around me failed to grasp. We talked a long time about the experience and what had happened to me in recent months, about the Ankh Society and running into Bilal al-Sheikh. But I didn't want to talk with him about the notion of divinity, so as not to offend his religious sensitivities. Finally, he looked at his watch.

"Time's gotten away from me." Then he went back to arranging some of the paintings and asked Janette for some old newspapers.

"You'll take the price I set," he said as he wrapped some of them up. He was serious, trying to avoid embarrassing me. "These are artworks and I'm buying them. Stop with this stupid pride." He pulled some money from his pocket and placed it on the side table. "If you say no, I'll just send it by mail transfer. It's only part of what you're owed. I'm an art lover, and I've got a right to my friend's works."

So far, he hadn't seen the portrait with the featureless face.

"Wait a second," I said, and I went into the boys' room and came back with it.

As soon as he saw it, he said, "That's mine."

"Anything but this one," I joked. "Leave it for a while; it keeps me busy. One day you'll find me knocking on your door and leaving it to you."

"Promise?" he said seriously.

"Promise."

He was overjoyed with the paintings.

"I always told you, you've got nothing but painting," he said as he headed to the door. "It's been a long time, but it doesn't matter. You took the first step."

I laughed. "Rida, I'm an amateur. This might be the last step. These are enough for me."

He stood in the middle of the living room and said, "What is the deal with you, brother? Just paint. Get to work. You're no good at anything else. Even if you paint dull, meaningless pictures, you'll enjoy it."

He had more faith in me than I did. At the door, he stopped again.

"Listen, if you do paint, I need to see it. I'll set up your first exhibition at my expense." As he descended the stairs, he said, "Who knows? Maybe these portraits will be worth big bucks one day."

"The joke's on you," I answered cynically. "There's no demand for these goods in this country."

I went back to the living room and saw the money on the table. It was hard to turn down, both because I needed it and because Rida had been so serious and insistent. I looked at it in wonder, but found no joy in my heart because of it. How much was it? A thousand pounds? Two thousand? I don't know. Maybe I'm not made to care about money. I'm only happy about it when I can buy painting supplies. I don't smoke, and my desire for food and clothing is limited. For me, money is a synonym for Janette, for household expenses. It's an odd part of my nature that I never examined, just left alone. Despite the poverty, I didn't need anything. I could live on anything—eat anything, wear anything. Money assumed some importance for me when I used to think about traveling. I thought about setting a sum aside so I could enjoy myself at the Red Sea or spend some time away in Matruh. But after living in al-Tur, I no longer wanted even that. Money was simply fuel, for the household, Janette's satisfaction, and the boys' happiness.

I went into the bedroom, where Janette was stretched out on the bed watching a soap opera. I left the money on the pillow. She looked at me and I saw tears glistening in her eyes. I thought it best to make a hasty retreat before the situation exploded, and I went to sit in my room to work on paintings for the art-supply shop.

# Yusuf Tadrus says:

Nagi Fahim, the owner of an art-supply shop, prepared year-end projects for the colleges of education and applied arts and sold them to the students. He offered me a huge range of projects and I chose the ones on the decorative arts. It was the first time I'd worked with gouache, and I took to it. Honestly, the material suits a poor artist working as a civil servant, who doesn't have enough money to buy other materials. The medium chose me. The serenity that suffused my spirit after the tempest of the self-portraiture helped me work for long stretches on these tedious paintings.

It wasn't all bad. Some of the pharaonic ornamentation stirred up a new sensitivity to painting—an internal tension. Sitting there painting endless frames of floral motifs and lotus flowers in all their variations makes you privy to the unlimited dimensions of a single element of nature. The experience endows you with a reflective sensibility, like those monastic ascetics of old. I communed with those images with patience, feeling that I'd been rescued from the monastery, and observed the endless facets of the motifs.

The ornamentation and graduation projects also gave me a chance to paint figures I never thought I'd paint: gazelles, birds, and winged bulls. The lines of a gazelle are simple, but painting it dozens of times in miniature has another flavor altogether, evoking its particular surroundings and the world of desert valleys and hilltops at dawn. It summons its unique elegance, giving you the feeling that you're there, standing on a hillock in the desert. The winged bulls of Assyrian art, the lions with human faces, falcons, and serpents—I painted all those creatures for hours on end, and they fertilized my existing imaginative images and sharpened my sense of the beings I'd kept company with in a period of my life. It stirred a profound sensitivity to images that had taken shape at a distance, without my knowledge.

In the silence of the long, exacting work, Janette moved about like she'd finally gotten what she wanted and had caged me. As long as I was doing something "useful" for the household—as long as I made money from the work to help with the expense of private tutors—it made her feel I'd become part of the fabric of the household, no longer that stranger who stood on the margins. I think that was her greatest victory.

Michel scored poorly on the matriculation exam, but it was enough to get him into the College of Tourism and Hotel Management as planned. His goal was clear: he would finish up the four years and travel. Where, he didn't know, but the older he got, the more outsized the idea became. He wouldn't be able to live here. This country reeks and he wanted to live where the air was clean. His taciturn nature and practical smarts wouldn't leave him prey to delusions like me. He knew very well what he wanted.

The fall came and he went to Fayoum to live next to the college. The flavor of life, its rhythms and rituals, changed. When one person leaves home, the others are left befuddled, uncertain how life should go on. It's not as fixed as they had imagined. Fadi was in his first year of high school and his troubles had begun. He looked at girls with the gusto of a small animal, and from the onset of puberty, he reveled in his body. He worked in the jewelers' district with his uncle and flirted with girls. I realized his path was plain. If he weren't killed in a fight over a girl, which happens a lot these days, he'd work in the jewelry business running a gold shop. I was in my midforties, and I'd begun to glimpse the first inklings of stability in my life and emotions.

I had to work hard, giving private lessons at the church and painting, to pay for Michel's college and board in Fayoum. At the beginning of the academic year, there were no graduation projects, so Nagi Fahim took advantage of my need for money by giving me pharaonic paintings on papyrus to copy, and portraits of "native" women in traditional garb, striking sexy poses and carrying earthenware jugs on their heads. He made posters of the illustrations and sold them. This work put me in a foul mood, and I started to feel put upon once I'd gotten all I could out of the experience.

Copying became incredibly tedious. I'd spend long hours coloring in pharaonic motifs. I'd imagine the ancient artist— no doubt he left such finishing touches to his underlings. I tried as much as possible to bear the load for the sake of the money Michel needed for his studies. You can't actually separate the good from the bad in the job. It was a single mass, like life. With difficulty, I endured the copying, but it helped me to know my temper and my goal. While copying all the pictures, I discovered I wasn't made for anything but painting. I shouldn't have left the College of Arts no matter what. I discovered my mistake. But life doesn't move backward. It's a single chance, and you either take it or miss it, you and your luck.

On those long nights I'd sit in the living room with a small table before me, painting the same creatures—the same birds, same feathers, endless lotuses—until my vision blurred and the shapes bled into each other. Under the sway of that never-ending repetition, the painter who had been buried by life's circumstances was reborn, though I wasn't conscious of it. I'd stretch out on the carpet in the living room, saturated with the smell of humidity and the walls, and feel I was as near to myself as possible. I'd get tired and go to bed, but as soon as I closed my eyes, the figures would spring up in my mind, the creatures arising from their repose into fearsome sizes, fused into a single mass. I paid them no mind, letting them frolic as they wished, but they swirled and filled my dreams. I'd wake up feeling I'd lived in another world, like I had a familiar spirit that visited unknown places. I knew, later, that those images were searching for an outlet for their existence, and then the day came when I made my first painting.

# Yusuf Tadrus says:

IT WAS A WINTER DAY I spent at home. Janette went to work in the morning, and Fadi was at school. I was alone. The sun was clouded over and on the balcony opposite me, a shawl was hung out on the clothesline. Blown by the wind, it formed undulating, fleeting shapes, a new one every moment. I thought about the power to produce new forms latent in everything around me; even the fixed features of the human face could not be encompassed with all their mutations. I felt the shawl was alive, speaking to me, and I wondered what made the shawl an inanimate being and the human a living being. A passing fancy, but it gripped me and I thought about it at length. The shawl loomed behind my thoughts, as if telling me to keep going. It's my madness that I yield to at times, in moments of silence, like a child at play.

I'm going to tell you about it in detail because I think that every detail in that day is significant. I know it's my deluded imagination, but let me finish my tale.

I thought the difference was the belief that the human being has a soul and the shawl doesn't. What I'm calling "soul" is my feelings and perception, those forces that delude a person into believing he's above nature. The human being has stripped the soul out of things and joined it to himself. Consciousness and feelings are distinctly human characteristics, but they don't make humans higher than anything. They're like the coarseness of a textile and its softness in the shawl, its flammability or receptivity to weaving, or any other characteristic that sets the shawl apart from other concrete things. Feelings and consciousness are simply natural characteristics of one of these concrete things, no different from the characteristics of rocks, plants, and marine creatures. What makes me call this a soul and elevate the status of humans while I see the shawl on the balcony opposite as lacking a soul?

Serenely lost in my thoughts, I told myself with certainty that a shawl moved by the wind on a winter day, with its woven texture, decorative flourishes, and shifting movement, had a soul like a human. Like a human being, the shawl is acted on by nature, regardless of the human being's activity and the shawl's passivity. The words *activity* and *passivity*, like *inertia* and *action*, are loaded terms, bent to the preferences of people. Maybe it goes back to a way of looking at existence. Civilizations marked by the will to control nature and forge it anew are inevitably partial to concepts like activeness, movement, and vitality. But a reflective civilization that sees human beings as part of nature and seeks to live in harmony with the universe would be partial to stillness, contemplation, and inaction. These are our terms; they're not about concrete things in nature, but reflect our own truth, not the truth of existent things. In general, a soul is a formal container for action—a form for the way a human being exists, and also for a shawl. Every being has a form for existence. It has a soul, if we recognize this soul as its form for existence.

Don't laugh, please. These thoughts were pleasurable, as if I were trying out thinking for the first time. I drank two cups of tea while reflecting on the movement of the shawl and trying to guess what form it would next take. My expectations were invariably foiled—it always undulated in a different way, tracing another figure, as if alerting me to the creative energy in everything, even in that small alley. I looked off the balcony: Amm Farag the carpenter hadn't opened his workshop today; the hairdresser on the corner was closed; the wind was audible as it whipped the walls; the sky was close and dark. You know, I saw in everything an endless potential to take a form that had never existed before, each form leaving behind another. This action of observing and thinking left me in awe at the exuberance of life and its creative capacity.

In the afternoon, Janette and Fadi returned, we ate, and I slept a little and then woke up with no desire to work on Nagi Fahim's paintings. I spent some time in silence reading out of an old magazine and watching the ads on television and a foreign movie about the forced resettlement of Africans in America in the sixteenth century. Displacement is a terrible thing. Snatching a man from his country is like uprooting a tree. The Africans were lost on the ship as if in another world, an anguish and intolerable terror in their eyes. These feelings of grief overwhelmed me and seemed to overpower the morning's reflections.

After Janette and Fadi went to sleep, I sat in the living room, scribbling on paper with charcoal. I heard a faint sound: raindrops with a rhythm like beads spilling onto the plastic tarp Janette had left over the laundry on the balcony. I followed the rhythm and tried to grasp the melody of it. A faint musical phrase that would fade, only to recreate itself in a different way. The rain picked up and the melody shifted; then it let up and the initial melody returned, so alluring and compelling I felt it was being played on an instrument. In that instant, I was struck by a palpable desire to paint, a desire like a physical urge—it was illumination, really, the riddle of life solved in that instant.

I don't want to discuss it. Just let me tell you what happened, and then we'll talk. I had some black paper left over from the student projects and a box of paints on a side table in the corner. I grabbed the brush and started working without knowing what I wanted to paint. The feel of the brush on the paper's surface was summoning the picture. Maybe I was thinking of painting the ship of Africans headed for America, which recalled the boats that cross the Nile in the spot where my brother, Michel, had died. Everything is linked by its own special code. The lines bent and formed a river teeming with vivid fish like in the works of the ancient artists. Then I painted a celebration, a coronation—I don't know exactly what. Like the mulid of the Virgin, but the Virgin was a queen sitting on a distant throne there in the upper part of the painting. The perspective different from that in Western paintings, created through proximity and distance, light and weight, cold and hot. It was created in a way I hadn't studied, like an intuition. I painted a clamor like the holiday throngs, and I painted lanterns, candles, an uproar. I was resurrecting a world seen for the first time. My hand worked of its own accord, and I was utterly transported, like I was bringing forth the worlds I'd sought, but they were not ready-made, those worlds that swam in my mind without me glimpsing them.

Once I ridiculed Rida Boulos when he said, "Paint your dreams, Yusuf." I thought he was joking, but he was on to something. In that moment, I was extracting the images from the reservoir of dreams. In one night, I painted seven pieces— can you believe it?—all strikingly similar and strikingly distinct. I painted the face of the ghoul, the truck that flattened me, as a caricature, as if it contained the weaving workshop within it, sparrows flying around, and Ghayath Street on Friday morning as the branches of the Christ's thorn swept over the wall of Dr. Taha al-Alfi's house. I found my hand weaving the birds I'd drawn for the students' projects, recreating them playfully as in dreams. The unattainable secret of my youth now poured forth under the brushstrokes. The world seemed so close. I could paint anything; I only had to fix the image in my mind and let it produce itself as it wished. I sat there until morning, the seven paintings arranged around me on the living-room chairs. When Fadi and then his mother got up, I didn't move from my spot. They looked curiously at this creature and the pictures surrounding him on the chairs.

At that moment, I could not go back to being a father, a husband, or an employee. I was another being. For a brief spell, I indulged myself, and Janette indulged me and let me be, preparing me breakfast and then going to work. I felt the intense solitude around me. A moment of clarity that isn't often repeated. The more I looked at the paintings, the greater my astonishment. Who painted these? Where did they come from?

I couldn't go to the school that day; couldn't pick up the chalk and lecture the children. I couldn't. I got dressed and left the house. The sunlight had a rare luminosity. The market was inundated with mud. The farmer women sat on the side of the road, having covered the mud with a layer of straw, and the baskets of vegetables were open, their colors freshly washed. People were lined up, crossing the small footpath toward the station tunnel.

I wandered aimlessly, nothing blocking me, giving my mood free rein to choose the places it wanted. I sat on the station platform, watching people getting on and off the provincial trains. Then I went and ate beans and falafel on al-Qantara Street and drank tea at a café in the alley. I wandered around the area I loved: the area of my childhood, Aziz Fahmi and Ghayath Streets. I entered the labyrinthine alleyways, looking adoringly at the doors and windows. The paper Ramadan decorations were dancing with the wind in the streets, and the rain made the alleys alien, like they were steeped in water. Open windows here and there, a faded wooden door with peeling paint, old, with an iron knocker in the shape of a clasping hand, until I reached the alley.

My feet led me to the source. The alley had been turned into warehouses again, as it had begun. I stood at the entrance, seeing rusty locks on the doors. Some of the windows were ajar. I saw the window with the iron bars that I used to swing from as a child. The rain had left a huge puddle in the middle of the alley. On mornings like this, I'd go with my mother to the sawmill, where we'd fetch sawdust to scatter next to the walls. I loved the smell of sawdust, and I wished I could hear the radio playing faintly from the living room. The sun hit the edge of a window on the left that was slightly ajar, and I saw a gray cat jump onto the windowsill and sit there, looking into the empty space, then cross through the open window inside. A mouse scampered next to the wall, and I followed it as it crossed the door, recalling the fear of Khawaga Tadrus. I heard the chirp of a bird perched on a piece of wood jutting out from the roof, surveying the scene from above.

Wandering those streets, I remembered that the room the cat had entered was Umm Bisa's. It was painted entirely in red. They said she consorted with the jinn. She had come with her husband, the truck driver, from the Khalafawi area of Cairo. She lived among us like she was from the alley. Sometimes I'd hear them saying that she sent her husband to sleep in the cab of the truck because one of the jinn was visiting her that night. She was a strange one. People from all over the city would come to her to have their palms or coffee grounds read. My mother saw her burying a small roll of fabric under the window—they said it was her son by one of the jinn, who would grow there, underground, to adulthood. I smiled when I remembered her anger. None could withstand it—it was the very definition of grotesque, a wholly misshapen face.

That morning, every detail was important, every passing memory brought an impression to life. I was communing with my absent self, the one that had gone so far away. The sight of the cat crossing to the inside wouldn't leave me. I wandered around the area of the Ahmadi Mosque. The streets were muddy, but the sunlight was pure gold. There was something magnificent in that day. Art gives you this union between the corporeal and the spiritual, the past and present. It's a moment in which time is assembled and shows itself to you, free of its fragmentation in our daily lives. I was as peaceful as if I'd found myself and gotten my wish. Every glimpse of my childhood helped me and granted me light.

Haven't you experienced an intense moment like that? A momentous juncture, like you were made of clay and then transformed into a being with a soul; you were a desiccated trunk, and then life pulsed in you and you felt the buds ready to bloom. Forgive the sentimentality, but it's the truth. I had a tough life, and my reward was readied for me on that morning, intense and vivid as the face of the Lord.

That day I understood that art didn't come from replicating figures like they taught us; it came from replicating the process of creation in nature. You want to know what I mean? Look at one of those shoddy statues in the public squares, and then take a long look at the sculptures of Rodin or Mahmoud Mukhtar or Henry Moore. You'll see the difference. Those works weren't created by the skill of the artist alone—they came out of his profound awareness of how creation works. Look at Moore's sculptures. They're born of a natural process of creation: gestation, dormancy, and failed attempts at being until that instant of the creative jolt, the spark that catches. In literature, haven't you often talked about the lengths Dostoevsky went to in drafting his manuscripts, how he tracked events around him, observed an execution, and involved himself in other proceedings he didn't know when and how he might use? I understood that. I had to follow the images. I wasn't mimicking nature. No, I just let nature do its thing.

# Yusuf Tadrus says:

DON'T IMAGINE SUCH MOMENTS LAST. They can't. A person would be utterly consumed if he remained in that state of agitation. Nature's merciful, and sly. The fading of that moment is a chance to choose: how will you make your way? What will you do when the spring stops bubbling? The choice is yours. The first time it's a gift, and after that comes the suffering. Attempting to recreate the experience is absurd—you're trying to relive what cannot be relived. You were given it once, to show you the way. The rest is down to your own efforts. Will you be able to create it again with patience and struggle? Or will you delude yourself with a false life? Live a brittle existence in an empty life? It's up to you.

I learned this over a full year of work, chasing that revelatory moment. Sometimes I'd catch a glimpse of it, when I was absorbed in painting, but soon enough it would recede. Flashes, no more than a glimpse. I'd revel in them, thinking them company for the road. The experience taught me not to stop, but to live. I shouldn't abandon painting no matter what happened. I had found my way.

So I painted incessantly. Even on those difficult days when it resisted me, I'd make sketches, recalling the feeling of camaraderie, painting, and drawing things closer to me. In that period, I learned my education was lacking so I studied the techniques of the masters. I copied so many paintings, from every school of art, from ancient civilizations to European arts throughout the ages. I reflected at length on the craft of the masters. I want to tell you something: the masters are masters in every age. With European modernism, their brilliance and refined human sensibility are especially apparent. Modernism was the striving of the great masters. It wasn't, like it is with us, an escape from the fundamental principles of art, a cloak to hide the painter's meager skills. I had to replicate these paintings to get to know their interior structure and how thought moves as the painting takes shape. You can't ever fully understand a painting until you copy it or mull over it for long stretches. Some silly conventions say that replication dilutes your own character, but no, it hones it. Your character is a fingerprint that can be neither acquired nor lost.

In the midst of all that, I had to carry on providing for the household. But when I found my way, the affairs of life were no longer burdensome. Go figure. They became instead an occasion for consciousness regained, a barrier between myself and the fantasies I vanished into. These boundaries are important. They keep you grounded in the thick of life without sliding into fantasy. Even more than that, every act acquired a distinct savor, even Fadi's refusal to go fetch the morning beans and my decision to go down every morning in pajamas to buy them myself. I came to know the sweetness of the morning bean errand. I got to know Amm Ali and we often chatted, and I learned of the ancient hearth where they stewed the beans near al-Sayyid al-Badawi. If you're attuned to happenings around you, everything has its own flavor; if you dig in your heels and resist, the harmony is broken and you're back in the void.

I stopped painting the student projects for Nagi Fahim's shop. They were exhausting and paid virtually nothing. Rida Boulos suggested I work with a translation office and I translated articles on everything, from birds' nests to active learning tools to the service economy, even the meaning of beauty in art. I took pleasure in it—I wanted to take a break from my fingers, which were always digging things up, and use my mind. Rida would visit occasionally to see the paintings and encourage me, telling me I'd accomplished something good. He said they combined a folkloric spirit with dream creatures, showing a touch of Islamic art's antipathy to empty space.

I came across a book on the Fayoum portraits and was as happy as if I'd found my heart's desire. I painted the faces nonstop, copying them all. I immersed myself in them and lived among them, as if I were fated to consort with faces, to struggle with them and love them. I have a genuine connection with the human face. Plunging into the world of the Fayoum portraits, I fell in love with Irini. I felt I'd seen her before, that there was some connection between us. Can you fall in love with the image of a woman who has been dead for nearly two thousand years? It was a light, soaring love, tinged with sadness at the thought that beauty can die. Everything can perish.

Art is a source of both grief and joy. It's like a port in a storm, or maybe an illusion necessary to confront the fear of nothingness that radiated from Irini's portrait, her wide black eyes and her stare, fixed on something outside the portrait. Painting faces has an unbearable drama. What happened to those faces I painted in my youth? What happened to those people? I wanted to see my paintings hung in parlors and know what happened to the people I'd painted.

There was something melancholy and compelling in Irini's picture. I built up a whole life for her, imagining her house and her father, the senior provincial official, her trousseau and her flawless body with its smooth litheness. I imagined her secret love for a priest, her impending marriage to a knight she did not love, and her grief that ate away at her body and hollowed it out, and how before her death, she sat for the artist to paint her portrait. Irini of the profound grief, solitude, and silent life. I painted her several times, and I understood the link between portraits and icons. I already knew it as a fact, but I understood the secret. These faces look at us from outside time, from within the nothingness we came from and to which we will depart. These faces contain a wisdom that slowly seeps into you, a captivating serenity and sadness. They hold the vexing equation and stare into us, but they no longer exist. Life and death coexist in the look in their eyes: the sorrow of not existing, but still looking out at life and knowing that it is more beautiful than anything else.

Never mind. I painted and learned. I was no longer searching for illumination. You know, if I'd been enthralled by the flash of illumination, everything would have been lost, but it was a kindness from the Lord. I could have been enthralled and thought myself inspired, rebuilding the myth I'd smashed. The mindfulness I'd acquired when painting my own face helped me, and you know my life is arid and the temptation of myths is great.

I continued painting, realizing that everything depended on patience and work and on heeding my inner self, there, where the images took shape. You have to approach them with caution and much patience to be able to create an impression. I didn't often hit the mark, but at certain moments a painting would arrive in which all the previous disappointments seemed to coalesce. I learned not to let failure bother me. A succession of failures—that's the only way to accomplish a good painting. An image forms itself and draws its weight from the repeated failures to paint it.

This is how the days passed. Rida Boulos was observing the experiment and made me meet him every week. If I missed it, he'd drop by before returning to Alexandria. He sat silently for long stretches in front of the paintings because, he said, he wanted to see how things would evolve.

"It's time, Yusuf," he said in the summer, perusing all the works. "We have to think of a way to exhibit all these paintings. Let me take care of it."

He called from Alexandria and said he'd spoken to an old friend at the College of Arts and showed him the portraits. He liked them, saying they'd make a great exhibit—one face painted dozens of times would be fantastic. But I refused to show the faces. They were less an experiment in art than an experiment in healing. We agreed I'd exhibit the new paintings in November at the Alexandria Atelier. Rida would cover all the expenses: the framing and the glass, and he'd send a company truck to take them to Alexandria.

Nothing can match the thrill of the first exhibition. It was the first time I saw Janette happy, like her life had borne fruit. She started thinking of a special gesture to offer visitors at the exhibit and finally hit on an idea: she bought chickpeas and chufa from down near al-Sayyid al-Badawi to offer to guests. It was a brilliant day, just our friends and the gallery visitors. We stayed at Rida's apartment in Sidi Bishr.

It was a lovely time, but frankly I hoped to sell some paintings. Remember, this was the first time I'd come into contact with the so-called art world, so don't be surprised by my naïveté. Days passed and nothing happened. There were a few words of encouragement in the guestbook I'd put next to the entrance; Rida paid me tribute and bought a couple of paintings, and that was it. To tell the truth, I was upset and almost lost my faith in what I had undergone in the recent past, but the Lord doesn't forget your brother Yusuf.

One day a young Chinese man and his wife came to the exhibit. Dressed in a suit, he looked like an employee at a company or embassy, I don't know. He leisurely wandered through the exhibit, stopping before each painting and commenting and explaining something to his wife. In the end, he came over and asked me who had done these paintings. I pointed to myself. Looking at me like an alien, he said in broken Arabic, "The paintings are pretty." He repeated it and trained all his energy on talking in strained Arabic about their complex composition, their mythical, dreamy sensibility, and their rich, fresh colors.

"They are genuine paintings," he said, looking at me in wonder.

I stored away the words, as they reverberated in my head: they are genuine paintings. It was enough, believe me, enough that they were genuine paintings. He bought three pieces and took my telephone number, saying he might visit me. It became a friendship that lasts to this day. Every time one of his friends comes who is interested in art, he brings them to my house on a narrow lane in Tanta.

I didn't return to Tanta with even a single painting. Rida Boulos insisted on keeping them with him in Alexandria, and anytime anyone wanted to buy one, he would send for me to come and spend a day with them. Rida was happier than I was, despite the health problems that had started plaguing him. A woman from Sweden bought five paintings, a Russian woman three. An Italian guy liked one picture and an old Japanese man bought one.

I no longer needed to work a second job—that was the most important thing. I went back to meeting Hazim al-Shirbini at the Palace of Culture, along with a group of young artists. Hazim was teaching painting at the College of Specific Education. I wasn't comfortable in that atmosphere around the young people. They were all focused on the latest fads and competitions sponsored by the Ministry of Culture—it was all about prizes and contests. A few times I met artists from Cairo who came to see Hazim, and one of them argued with me about my disregard for the visual landscape—meaning I should paint cafés, streets, microbus stations, train platforms. That's something for fans of history and documentarians, or someone who finds a passion in painting reality and sees meaning behind the details of the landscape, giving us scenes like Van Gogh's night café or a billiard parlor where the table is laid out like a coffin. Artists of genius who take the visual landscape as their subject imprint their spirit on it and create it anew. You don't see fields in Van Gogh's paintings, you see vastness and an incandescent desire; you don't see a family actually eating potatoes, but a dream of a family eating potatoes. That's a singular kind of artist, and really, the artist doesn't choose his subject. It chooses him.

This was in the first burst of enthusiasm. I thought I had become an artist and I could take my paintings to state-sponsored exhibitions and see them acquired and collected like those of other artists. Here, though, I saw the other side of the art world. They stood against me in everything, showing only one of my paintings at the national exhibit and then ignoring me. I learned that world didn't suit my life. I'd grown up. My son Michel had graduated from the College of Tourism and was preparing to travel to America, where he'd live a few years and come back with a slender, kind girl and marry her here at the Church of the Archangel. God bless him, he wanted to make his dear mother happy, but he delighted me along with her.

My life changed. Whatever happened, I wouldn't let anything ruffle its serenity. Even if my paintings were just ordinary, I'd keep painting as long as it held something that bound me to my depths. That was the most important decision I made then, and without it, things could not have continued: I will not stop painting. I worked even harder, painted more pieces, had three more shows, and paid no mind to anything. That's how your brother Yusuf became an old man, no longer able to compete with anyone or scrap over exhibits, positions, and other things artists concern themselves with. I was fed up with that and hated it. I had to live my life elsewhere in peace and paint whatever pictures I had left in me.

# Yusuf Tadrus says:

I KNOW NOW THAT THE only woman who could have put up with me is Janette. It's she who took the gamble and descended into hell. She bore it all and made everything, and despite our stormy life, she remained my companion, mother, lover, and enemy—in short, life. Now her jealousy has cooled and her feelings for me have softened, and she's begun to feel companionable.

I discovered the wisdom in Coptic marriage and understood it. Our way of marriage suits the spirit of the religion of the cross. Even if you don't love your wife and your life is miserable, you must carry your cross, for therein lies salvation. Carrying it will grant you qualities you appreciate. With time, a spirit of concord is revealed; something good will grow in the blackness and misery, and in the end you'll find comfort in fellowship. You see many old couples on their way to church, leaning on each other. You don't know how their life began—maybe it began in love and continued in monotony, and then violence, and afterward hatred, peace, acceptance, and concord. In the end is comfort and peace. It's the same long journey of human growth and self-discovery.

I know I've become conservative. I see that a man won't grow up if he's constantly moving from breast to breast—he'll get more and more juvenile—so I'm no longer an advocate of divorce. You remember a long time ago, when I told you about the cathedral, the sweet girls and blooming boys, and the ruined life? Remember how angry I was that religious tradition denied them a life by forbidding divorce? Now I think otherwise. You'll say I'm against freedom and the church has to find a way to solve the problem. But no, I'm no longer convinced it will solve the problem. Every relationship at some point becomes a disappointment. If we allow divorce, most relationships will end in it, and no one will be able to understand the self, find maturity, and know what it means to live.

Janette's my companion now. When she sees me sitting stiffly in front of a painting, she tells me, "What, Yusuf? What's wrong, brother?" Another mother—that's how it ended up. Don't laugh at me. Believe me, everything happened so I could produce these paintings, this endless parade of cats, fish, humble families, and celebrations.

Michel has lived in America for two years. He had his first child, Mina. Your brother Yusuf Tadrus has become an old man with grandkids. Imagine: me, a grandfather! Michel came at Christmas, leaving his American wife here with his son and returning to finish up the citizenship process. I no longer have a job, and spend my time with Mina.

It's amazing to see your grandchildren. It's really like they say, your love for grandkids is stronger than your love for your kids. Don't tell me I've never loved anyone. The boy is my life now. I call him Mimi and I laugh with his mother. We chat about life and its vicissitudes. His hair is blond and soft, not like my coarse blond hair. His fine hair flutters on his forehead. His face is round, not the oval shape and sharp lines of your brother Yusuf's face. He has only this angular nose, that's what makes me worry for him.

I spend most of my time with him and teach him things—balcony, window, Umm Muhammad, Umm Maryam, carpenter, barber—and we laugh. It seems the Lord is pleased with me, finally. He was saving some delight for me for the end of life. But the fear resides in my heart all the same, a dark night. I fear it and its eternality; it still plagues me. Do you think it will melt away when I cross the ocean and lie there in the sun on the beach? Maybe it will. Maybe fear is a feature of this place. Maybe it will cease there.

Don't look so surprised. I'm going in June. I'll fly across the ocean to the other side, where the sun sets. There I'll live awhile, my mind at ease, far from all of you, far from the darkness I've always inhabited. There I'll be able to sleep a little in the sun. I'll leave you here alone to walk these dingy streets and remember you as you tend to your pictures and stories like a shepherd in the hills waiting in vain for grace.

Listen, if circumstances permit, I'll send you an invitation to visit me, but you've got to stop with your foolishness. Stop prattling on about how your life is a shambles here and will be in shambles wherever you go. Believe me, this is foolish talk. As long as you can draw breath, there is potential for movement, something else to throw yourself into. As for me, I still have time to travel there and play with Mina on the shore. I can take a short break from the fear and this darkness.

Tell me, for God's sake, when will the light shine on this country?